SAVING SALLY

AND OTHER MISHAPS

Lorretta Clarke

PUBLISHER'S NOTE
This is a work of fiction. Names, characters, places and incidents either are the
product of the author's imagination or are used fictitiously, and any resemblance
to actual persons, living or dead, business establishments, events, or locales are
entirely coincidental.

ISBN No: 978-0990974703 (Matthews Clarke Publishing)

Many thanks to all the people who have supported me throughout writing this book particularly to Laura Moorehead-Clarke and Sheila Clarke. To the Matthews and Smith families. To my husband, Steve who encourages me in everything I do. And lastly to Madelyn who has the most beautiful eyes, with which I used to make the cover of this book.

1

The sun rose swiftly from behind the mountain on the other side of the bay, resuscitating the monochromatic hills into a breath of color and replacing the cool breeze with warm pockets of still, lifeless air. Wearing a black, designer gym top and shorts, 32 year-old Sally Pringle ran along the path of the delta, gripping a water bottle in one hand and a set of house keys in the other. She glanced at the sun and already felt its intensity. If only she hadn't had that phone call, she would've been done by now. Eager to get the run over with, she widened her stride and headed towards Fenton's town center.

A fully loaded container ship glided swiftly and silently by. Its destination bringing further expansion to Ashwood, the city on the other side of the mountain. Ashwood, the hottest destination for young working couples seeking their first family home was, until four years ago, a sleepy backwater. But then a wave of soaring house prices made the long commute to San Francisco suddenly tolerable. Gone are the ranches, the winding tree-lined roads and the town center.

Now Ashwood is a modern metropolis with a huge indoor shopping mall at its center, a multi-screen cinema and a new 2,000 unit housing development. By comparison, Fenton seemed a world away. Over time, some businesses had changed from their origins of 1860. A grocery store had become a hardware store and the post office was now a hair salon. And while some thought that Fenton looked neglected and rundown, others were comforted by the fact that some things remained the same. But no-one doubted that Fenton was living on borrowed time and one day, it too, would be at the mercy of the bulldozer. For the past couple of months, there had been a steady stream of proposals for a new 'Fenton' travelling across the mayor's desk. It would only take a few poorly advertised public meetings together with a few bribes of certain key officials and it would all be gone in the blink of an eye. Already changing the landscape was a new housing development on the edge of town. Sally, like most of Fenton's residents, vehemently opposed any expansion or modernization to the town, fearing that once it started, it would be hard to stop and Fenton would become as characterless as its neighbor. Although a relative newcomer herself, she didn't want others coming here spoiling the idyllic life she had discovered.

Fenton is situated 50 miles east of San Francisco, away from the fogbank but close enough if you needed the fix of a bigger city. Its temperate weather allows outside activity year round and Sally usually ran six miles every morning. But for the past two weeks the weather had been unusually hot. She had cut her running time down to a meager 30 minutes, but even this was proving a struggle today. So far she had only run a mile and was already weary and breathless, but she pushed on regardless. Crisp brown leaves crunched underfoot and the pungent smell of tar rising from steam on the path stifled her. Her legs felt heavy, as though she were running through deep sand; every breath resented by her lungs. Sweat spat from her hair, ran down her body and dripped into her eyes. She wiped them clear with her forearm smearing the salty moisture across her fair, now sun burnt face. Gasping for air she forced a couple of deep, long breaths into her body. Then suddenly, as if she'd been given access to an extra pair of lungs, the tightness in her chest relented and her stride became more fluid. She had caught her second wind.

Sally nodded to the people as they passed by, among them cyclists, walkers and runners. In the distance, she recognized the hefty blonde haired woman with the Dalmatian. As she neared, Sally could see that her plump face was red with exertion. She ran erratically, being pulled along by her dog.

Fenton's inhabitants were split into two socio-economic groups: those whose families had lived here for generations and others who had been lured from the City by lower house prices and a higher standard of living during the '80s housing boom. The latter were still treated with some animosity. Their sudden appearance had escalated house prices to such levels that the offspring of the people already here were unable to afford them. Many had either doubled up with their parents, or had simply left the area altogether. Another bone of contention was the fact that most of the 'newcomers' worked in San Francisco and contributed little to the local economy. Like oil and water, the two groups rarely mixed and were easily identified by the quality of their cars, clothes and the speed with which they moved. Now the latest housing development threatened a new wave of immigration.

Dressed in gray, washed out flannel shorts and a white clinging T-shirt, Sally presumed the woman with the dog belonged to the former group. Her breasts rolled erratically from side to side from the inadequate support of an exercise bra. Sally's assumption was further confirmed because the woman took time to acknowledge her as she passed by, another thing she loved about Fenton.

Fast approaching, another runner, this time a man she hadn't seen before. He wore a dark blue vest, black soccer shorts and was running at Olympic speed. "There are two categories of men in the world," Louise Stanton's words suddenly sprang to Sally's mind. "Good bodies and brains. And they just don't exist in the same man," she'd said, hiccupping, drunk at Sally and John's wedding. "One you play around with, the other you marry." Sally acknowledged that intelligence, drive and loyalty were qualities that had attracted her to John. It wasn't that she found muscular men unattractive, she just assumed that guys who spent a lot of time bulking up must be narcissistic. So, in essence, she supposed she agreed with Louise, although her friend was hardly an authority on the matter, since she was just going through her third divorce.

The man running towards her was about 5'10" and although he was not of bodybuilding proportions had a wide chest. His head was shaved, and he had a swarthy complexion. By Louise's definition, he leaned more towards the 'play around with group' than the 'marrying kind', because Sally figured he must be a fitness fanatic to run at such a pace. Nevertheless, there was something compelling about him. His firm cheek muscles and pronounced intelligent brow gave him a commanding presence. Maybe an officer in the military, she pondered. Only a few yards away now, his eyes seemed fixed on hers, his stare excruciatingly pointed and threatening.

He ran straight at her. To avoid colliding, she jumped out of his way, spun around and watched him disappear into the distance. She bent over winded, keeping an eye on the man, wondering what was up with him. *If she hadn't moved out of his way....what a jerk.* After catching her breath she straightened, swallowed some water, and continued her run.

As Sally picked up speed again, she approached the newly erected park bench where she read ... *parks development*, the last words belonging to a long inscription on it. Over the past few days, she'd picked up snippets of information as she ran by. The bench was dedicated to Fred Patchett, for his lifetime achievement to the park's development. He'd died last year at the age of 73. She thought this sort of gesture pointless. Fred was dead and had never known about the bench and anyone using it would probably never give Fred a second thought.

Finally, she turned into the thick, oak canopied path that led to the town's center, her favorite part of her run. She was gratified by the cooler air and the shafts of sunlight bursting through the trees, revealing dust particles dancing in their path. It was so peaceful that the loudest noise she heard was her own breathing. Birds, mainly starlings and yellow breasted finches, flew between the trees and the ground, making the most of the irrigated grass. Squirrels scurried under walnut trees unconcerned by her presence or the busy road ahead. Crazy Alice, who regularly fed the birds, sat on a bench at the edge of the path. She threw small pieces of bread while chuckling and talking incoherently to the birds, as they fluttered and fought over the scraps of bread. Suddenly noticing Sally, she shouted "what you doing that for, silly!" When she didn't respond, Alice simply dismissed her with a flick of her hand and returned her attention to the birds. The peaceful sounds of nature drifted away, replaced by traffic noise, exhaust fumes and the sun's penetrating heat as she reached the highway. She pressed the crosswalk button and waited for the lights to change. After swallowing the remains of her water she threw the empty bottle into a trashcan and ran across the street.

On the corner of First and Main was Fenton's only hotel. Built in 1861, 'The Railway Station,' was an enigma since there had never been a railway through Fenton. There had been plenty of stories surrounding it, most based around corrupt city officials at the time of its construction. The commonly accepted but unofficial version was that the mayor of the time, the honorable Dr Wilkes, suggested that the railway might be persuaded to come to Fenton, if it already had a station. Of course, it was a ridiculous scenario but added to the town's eccentricity and was a draw for tourists.

At the next block Sally zigzagged around the back of a silver Porsche parked outside of 'Jeremiah's Watering Hole,' the town's oldest and most notorious bar. The car's engine purred away and the driver's door lay wide open. Despite widespread disapproval from Fenton's senior inhabitants, 'The Hole,' had started selling coffee in the mornings. "Keeping drunks wide awake," they'd carp. Proving that no matter how positive, the older residents would always resent change, believing that anything new must be directly linked to the 'newcomers', and so couldn't be good. Any moment, a coffee addicted commuter would run out, jump into the car and start their long, slow journey to San Francisco. Sally felt lucky that she'd been able to give up work after she'd moved to Fenton, some four years ago.

Passing the empty tables and chairs outside 'The Hole,' Sally started her steep ascent towards the 'new housing development,' which hardly deserved its name since it was at least 20 years old. The official name was 'High Bank' but few people ever called it that. She wondered what the locals would call the town's newest development on Jeremiah's Hill, once completed. Her calf muscles tightened and once again, her breathing slipped from its comfort zone, as she felt the full impact of the hill. Winded, she reached Third and backed up against the street sign.

Glancing left, she spotted the man who had almost run into her. He jogged on the spot waiting for a gap in the traffic. He looked harmless now, just a regular guy enjoying his morning run. His ordinariness made her feel silly about her reaction earlier. For all she knew, the guy could be shortsighted. She felt miffed though, that he'd made it up from the delta so quickly, despite having a much longer route and showing no apparent sign of fatigue. The man waited for the last car in a line of traffic to pass, then ran across the road, disappearing up the next block with an enviable lightness to his step. Sighing, Sally dragged herself from the post and waited for the same car to pass. Worn out and de-motivated she strolled across the road and continued up Main, thinking that maybe she'd badger John into joining a gym.

2

Helen Pearce's house was one of the 'new houses' on High Bank, thrown up during the short, sharp economic boom of the mid '80s. It had a mishmash of styles, a traditional ranch, covered with stucco and fake, dark wood Victorian trimmings. John had joked that the architect must have been on something when he'd designed it. Sally thought it contradicted Helen's fanatical sense of tidiness and order.

The front door was open; Sally pushed it wider and stepped into the hallway. "Hello!" she hollered to the women who were sitting around a coffee table in the living room.

"Shssss," they replied. Helen waved her over. She and Rachael Brookstone, were listening to their friend, Joan Hammond who sat on a high-backed chair, and read aloud from a green binder.

"Alex wore a powder blue strapless gown. She glided into the room ..."

Sally left the door as she had found it, slipped off her sneakers and made her way over to them. Sweaty from her run, and not daring to sit on the couch, she sat down on the white carpet, mouthing a "hi" to Helen and Rachael. Rachael raised her hand in greeting, her eyes not wavering from Joan. Helen rose from the couch, headed down the hallway and reappeared moments later with a folded towel for her.

"Thanks," Sally whispered, slipping it beneath her.

Helen had held this reading/writing group for approximately four years. Occasionally, someone read something they'd written, discuss a book or a recently released film, but more often than not the conversation would turn to local gossip. If it weren't for Helen's direction, Sally suspected that the group would have disbanded years ago.

"She flushed and drifted to the balcony," Joan continued.

Sally groaned to herself.

Joan sat perfectly straight in her chair and as always was immaculately turned out. She wore a simple red cotton dress and red leather flats. Not a hair out of place, she held the green binder with beautifully manicured hands. She addressed the other women in a soft, expectant manner, more befitting a high-class aristocratic lady than a middle-class suburban woman.

Joan had been raised in one of those all white upper middle-class families, the kind that thought they belonged to an even higher social class than they were. As a young adult, she had little experience of the world beyond her parent's country club. And although she would go to the ends of the earth to help a friend, she always spoke her mind with

10

fervent honesty which was often met with contempt, given her limited life experience. Even her writing emulated her narrow, sheltered life and this piece sounded like a bad version of 'Gone with the Wind.'

"… And for a moment she lost sight of him. Then from nowhere …"

She had been married to Eric Hammond for more than 30 years. They had one son, Joseph an architect, who lived in San Francisco. The group had surmised from snippets of information given by her over the years, that he was gay, though none of them had actually met him, and given Joan's conservative, religious background, no-one dared to suggest it.

Sally caught Rachael's eye and smiled. She sat on the couch nearest the window. Her long, straight, strawberry-blonde hair glowed red where the sun caught it. She was in her late 20's and had been married a couple of years to a local landscape gardener. The couple lived frugally in a small, old Victorian house with his mother, which Rachael seemed perfectly happy about. In fact, she was one of those maddening individuals who wore a permanent, contended smile no matter what life threw at her. It was as though she possessed an extra set of happy genes. Sally had never seen her upset nor heard her complain about anything. And she certainly had a gift for writing, her genre was children's short stories. Her last piece was about a mindreading dragonfly, which flew from person to person during a church garden fete. Helen, the most accomplished amongst them, thought Rachael stood a good chance in getting her work published, but so far she hadn't taken up Helen's offer to help get it to market. Sally thought it a crime not to capitalize on her gift, particularly since the couple were so hard up for money. She was six months pregnant and had an enviable glow about her. Maybe she should consider fertility treatment, Sally thought. After all, she and John had been trying to start a family for the best part of two years.

"Coffee, Sally?" Helen asked.

"Oh, no thank you."

Joan stopped reading and frowned at them.

"Oh, sorry Joan, I didn't mean to interrupt, please carry on."

After sighing, Joan continued. "She felt awkward and angry that he had the audacity to speak to her while she stood beside her husband …"

Helen rolled her eyes at Sally. Back in the early days, she had attempted to coach Joan on her writing, particularly on style, hoping at least to bring her into the current century. But she quickly discovered that Joan couldn't take criticism as easily as she could dish it out.

Helen's long, black, curly hair bounced as she sat back into the couch. Their host had just celebrated her 20th wedding anniversary to her second husband, Frank. She left her first husband after only 18 months of marriage, bearing a six-month-old baby, two broken ribs, and a black eye. She'd once said that she'd been glad her first marriage had fallen to such desperate levels, because she would probably have stayed in the unhappy marriage for the sake of her son Mark, and would, therefore, had not met Frank.

Sally and John had first met the Pearce's through a newcomers meeting at the local Presbyterian Church. Until recently, they'd met on a regular basis for dinner and Helen had become Sally's closest friend and confidant. They were empty nesters; Mark, a civil engineer lives in New York and Bruce is at the University of California San Francisco, studying biochemistry. Sally envied Helen's creative flair and greatly admired her confidence. She regarded her almost like a surrogate mother, often seeking her advice, even though her friend was only nine years her senior.

Helen bent forward and picked up a cookie, inadvertently nudging the plate. The china clattered against the glass tabletop. The coffee table, yet another piece of furniture she had recently bought, was somewhat avant-garde. It had a steel pyramid structure underneath, meeting the glass top at its apex. Sally glanced around the room, thinking that the inside of the house was beginning to look as confused as the outside. The couch was a Chesterfield, the high-backed chair, a Queen Anne copy and the fireplace was decorated with dark Spanish wood. Lately, it seemed that every time she stepped inside the house Helen had bought something new, sometimes replacing perfectly good furniture. *Why had she suddenly started buying all this stuff. Was it a symptom of something?* It was true that Helen had been complaining about Frank lately. She'd moaned about his laziness, that he didn't want to do anything with her. Sally wondered whether buying the furniture was her way of filling this void. Still, she thought, the coffee table was one of her better purchases.

"Hi guys! Sorry I'm late!" bellowed a voice from the front door. A waft of hot air rolled into the cool air-conditioned room, as Marie unsuccessfully tried to lift her baby's stroller into the hallway. Helen went to help.

13

Joan stopped reading again and stung the air with another sigh.

Helen picked up the front of the stroller and helped lift it inside.

"Oh, thanks Helen."

"They glided onto the …" Joan continued.

Marie pushed her sleeping son into the corner of the hallway and approached them, straightening herself with an affectionate hand to her back.

"Sally, please don't tell me you've been running in this heat," Marie bellowed. "Gosh, and your face has caught the sun too!"

Not wanting to interrupt Joan, Sally just smiled. Nevertheless, she broke off reading again and gave Marie a good, slow, critical scan, then continued, "She jumped into the back of the car, and with tears in her eyes, the chauffeur drove her home …"

Marie dropped next to Rachael on the couch and Helen parked herself on one of its arms. Just turned 32, Marie Thomson had been adding to the world's population since she was 18 years old. She had four children, three girls and a boy. By her own admission she needed to lose about 30 lbs. As usual, she was dressed in an unflattering baggy t-shirt and blue, faded jeans. Sally realized why Joan had stared at her so disapprovingly. Her top had dried milk stains on it and her brown, shoulder length hair stuck out at one side. Sally presumed that she'd either missed that part of her hair in a frantic comb through that morning, or she'd driven with her van's window down.

"Well, that's as far as I've got," Joan said, wrapping up.

14

"Oh, well done!" Sally said truthfully, referring more to her effort, than content.

"It's really coming along," Rachael said.

"Thanks," Joan beamed appreciatively.

Naturally, the piece should have been critiqued but as no one dared, an awkward silence filled the room, leaving the women glancing at each other with stilted grins. The grandfather clock on the opposite side of the room chimed 10:00 am, adding even more tension to the air.

"Coffee anyone," Helen asked, finally breaking the silence. She placed the dirty cups on the tray, and headed to the kitchen.

"Are you alright?" Rachael asked Marie. She must also have noticed her shabby appearance.

"Oh yes, yes I'm fine," Marie said. "I'm so spaced out lately. The constant noise level at home is driving me crazy. And getting the kids ready for school," she said, rolling her eyes. "It's the same thing every, single morning. They can't find this! They can't find that! And to top it all, the oldest has just started high school. I spend the entire morning in the van, shuttling between schools!" She seemed defeated and slightly tearful. There were murmurs of sympathy all around.

But Sally didn't give much credence to Marie's grumbling. It was obvious that she wouldn't have it any other way. Sally thought she was just having a bad day.

"Anyway," she continued. "You don't want to hear about my petty woes. Did any of you hear about the shootings?"

"The what?" Sally asked. "What shootings?"

"Oh, you mean the student pranks," Rachael said dismissively. "Apparently, some high school kids have been shooting BB guns at houses in the neighborhood. They've smashed some windows and scared a few people."

"That's terrible," Joan said.

Marie shuffled to the edge of the couch and helped herself to a cookie. "Well, I bumped into Doreen Anderson this morning. She said at least one of the shootings, last Tuesday's I think she said, wasn't from a BB gun, but from a rifle."

"No!" Joan gasped.

"Oh, she's full of hot air," Sally said. "Doreen Anderson's hardly a reliable source. Anyway, where did she say she heard that?"

"She said she'd read it in the 'Tribune' this morning."

Helen returned from the kitchen with a tray stacked with fresh cups and a coffeepot.

Marie got up and scanned the room. "Hey Helen, have you got today's Tribune?" Helen placed the tray on the coffee table and Rachel helped to spread out the cups.

"Yes, in the magazine rack, over there, by the side of the fireplace. Why?"

"There's an article in it about some shootings." Marie sorted through the rack. "Here it is. Right on the front page." She held up the paper for them to see.

'Shootings in Fenton!' Sally noted.

" 'Last week,' " Marie read. " 'Fenton Police received 911 calls from frantic residents reporting that they had been shot at through their windows. Following an investigation, it was

16

revealed that the shots were fired from BB guns, and believed to be the result of a high school prank.' "

" 'However, this week the Fenton Police Department issued a new statement to the 'Tribune' indicating that at least two of these incidents were not the result of BB guns, but were shots fired from a small caliber rifle.' "

"Oh!" Sally gasped.

" 'Sheriff Laker of the Fenton Police Department stated that he regarded these incidents as serious. He added that he'd been concerned about the increase in serious crimes for quite some time. He asked for the residents of Fenton to be vigilant and to call the Police Department if they see anything suspicious.' "

"Why haven't I heard anything about this?" Sally asked. "When did all this start?"

"A couple of weeks ago." Marie leafed through the paper. "I think the police have been trying to keep a lid on it. Here, there's more. 'In response to the Sheriff's statement, Mayor McKinley stated that although there had been an increase in crime over the last year, statistics show that in real terms, crime has decreased in correlation to the increase in population to the area. Mayor McKinley, the Tribune reports, was a vehement supporter of the recent housing expansion project.' "

"Well, that's put an end to his political career," Joan mocked.

Sally recalled that McKinley had recently been accused of being in the pockets of housing developers and some local realtors. Despite widespread opposition to the project, the developers had managed to obtain permits by using vague

17

language and confusing tactics during public meetings. She agreed with Joan, McKinley was history.

Joan took the paper from Marie and scanned the article herself. "It's a bit worrying though, don't you think? I mean, shootings, here of all places."

Helen poured the coffee. "I don't think you should believe everything you read in the newspapers, particularly a small one like the Tribune. Local reporters are notorious for blowing things out of proportion. Although, it wouldn't surprise me if some organization's behind it."

"What do you mean? What kind of organization?" Sally asked.

"Well, environmentalists for one, trying to stop the new housing project." Helen replaced the coffeepot on the tray.

"You really think there could be a conspiracy to stop the new housing development?" Rachael asked.

"Well, some people still feel resentment over the last development and that was over 20 years ago. I still get disapproving looks when I tell people which street I live on. What better way to scare off prospective bankers, investors and buyers, than a bit of vandalism. But, speaking of conspiracies.." Helen strolled over to the other side of the room. "I've been clearing out the basement lately and found an old story I'd written a few years back."

"Oh really, what kind of story?" Joan asked.

"A murder mystery." Helen pulled out a large, tatty-looking black notebook from the top shelf of a bookcase. "Would you like to hear some of it?"

Of course everyone did. Joan folded the newspaper, replaced it in the rack and quickly returned to her seat.

Helen sat down on the stone hearth and leafed through the notebook, while filling them in on the background. "It's set in a suburban town called Brownsville. It's about a young successful couple with everything going for them. Married for 15 years, two small children, big house, nice cars, all the trappings. The husband's an investment banker but he makes a bad investment decision, losing his employers a considerable amount of money. James, the husband tries to recover his position by persuading the bank to invest in a high-risk, quick return venture, but this also turns sour. During all this, he falls for his secretary, Lisa. From the beginning she'd known about his position, and kindly offers support and a sympathetic ear. Anyway, one thing leads to another and they have an affair."

"But, what about his wife?" Joan interrupted. "Doesn't she support him?"

"She doesn't know. They were both brought up in upper-class families, where the man discusses nothing about business with his wife. So naturally, their marriage functioned the same way."

Joan, however, continued to frown so Helen explained further. "In high society, it's considered uncivilized to discuss money matters with family members. Their relationship was such that she ran the house and raised the children, while he took care of money and business."

"But Helen, as you know, I am familiar with the ways of high society and I think it highly unlikely that a wife wouldn't have suspected that her husband was having problems at work." She glanced around the other women

19

looking for signs of support. "Well, I would know if Eric was having problems at work."

A loud groan came from Marie. Sally wished Joan would shut up and let Helen begin reading.

"Don't get me wrong, Helen, I'm not criticizing your work. We all know that you're such a talented writer. I just think it's an unlikely scenario. That's all."

"Thanks for pointing it out to me," Helen said diplomatically. "I'll bear that in mind when I start editing."

"Let's hear more," Rachael said, glancing at her watch. "I've got to run in a few minutes."

"Well, as I said, James and his secretary are having an affair. His company suggests that he either resign or move to a lateral position, which in reality translates to a demotion. To buy himself enough time to work out his next move, he accepts the position. In the meantime, he purchases an apartment in the city for himself and his secretary. He's torn between wanting to live full time with Lisa and giving up his extravagant lifestyle, which he'd inherited from his wife. So instead of divorce, he decides to have her murdered."

"No, no, I'm sorry," Joan exclaimed. She sat up stiffly, shaking her head. "It's just not plausible."

"Well," Helen said. "Why don't …"

But it was too late, Joan had already taken a large intake of breath. "If they had been married for 15 years and had what you portray, a good relationship, then I can't believe that the husband wouldn't have discussed his problems at home. After all, 15 years is a long time to live with someone and not suspect that something's wrong." Joan tilted her head to one side. "I think the wife would have guessed that her husband was having problems at work and confronted him about it, long before he had the opportunity to turn his attention to another woman."

"Oh, for heaven's sake!" Marie yelled.

"I mean, you don't live with someone all that time without knowing things like that," Joan continued.

"But…" Helen tried to interject.

"And if he's having an affair, there would be warning signs; lipstick on his shirts, smell of perfume," Joan rattled on. "You just would know. No, I'm sorry Helen, I have to say, your work is usually excellent, but I really think you need to rethink this storyline. It's just not normal for a wife not to know that something's amiss. After all, we all know," she continued in a soft, belittling voice, "that good writing is based on real life situations."

Sally glanced at Helen. Her expression was totally undecipherable. But Sally could well imagine what was going through her mind, after patiently listening to Joan's drivel for the last half an hour.

"I think it's great so far," Marie said. "I don't wear lipstick or perfume."

"Marie," Joan declared, using her most regal voice. "I don't think that Helen is portraying someone like you. Normally people do wear makeup and perfume."

"Huh? And you would know what normal is!" Marie snapped. Surprised by her sudden outburst, everyone turned to her. "The person that demands her husband take a shower every night before he gets into bed with her. You call that normal!"

"Well that Marie, was totally uncalled for!" Joan said affronted.

"Now, come on girls, let's hear some more of Helen's story," Rachel pleaded, trying to defuse the situation.

Joan fell silent, now seemingly lost for words.

Helen continued. "As I said. This is just a rough draft. Susan's and James's characters and their relationship will be revealed as the story progresses. 'The leaves of autumn ...'"

Still stunned, a red faced Joan stared into space. Marie sat with her elbow on the arm of the couch and her cheek perched on her fist. She stared at the floor as Helen read her story. Sally spotted another expression on Marie's face. Along with tired and tearful, she now also looked regretful.

3

On her way home, Sally pondered Helen's story. Although she said it was a rough draft, she'd already created a captivating story. The plot was intriguing and her characters were pretty well developed. She promised to give each of them a copy at the next meeting.

Then she considered Joan's objection to the couple's relationship in the story. Like Sally, she'd obviously compared her own relationship with her husband, with the one portrayed by Helen. Sally, however, didn't share Joan's view. She believed that people were unpredictable. It was only a month ago that Ellie Baxter, Sally's closest childhood friend, told her that she had discovered her husband had been having an affair throughout the entire duration of their six year marriage. As a managing consultant, her husband spent long periods away from home, so was well able to keep the affair under wraps. Ellie had only found out about it when he'd slipped up during a heated argument. However, Joan and Eric's lives were so scheduled, that such a scenario would seem improbable. Sally found it odd how she would rush back to her house in case Eric called when the group met on Tuesdays, particularly in the age of the cell phone. But hey, she thought, they'd been married for more than 30 years, so who was she to criticize. Sally's only objection to the story was that it was set in a small suburban town like Fenton. Its fast pace, together with a murder plot, seemed more fitting to a much larger town or city.

Turning the corner of her street, she sighed at the sight of the contractor's trucks parked outside her house. The remodel, near completion, was six months over schedule and any degree of excitement she had felt at the beginning had gone. Still, she'd be glad to see the back of it.

A warm breeze shook the liquid amber tree as she strolled past her neighbor's garden. The crisp brown leaves fell to the ground as silent as snowflakes. Like her own, the Grainger's house was one of the few original houses on the street. Tom and Kath had lived there since it had been built and would probably be there until they died. The rancher was encircled by a porch, a large lawn and a white picket fence. She was in no doubt that one day it would be torn down and replaced by a large, two story house, when the Grainger's had gone. Sadly, it seemed the way the whole neighborhood was heading.

Sally and John had discovered Fenton five years ago, while on their way to a hike. Often noticing the villages' church spire from the freeway whenever they passed that way, she'd persuaded him to exit on the pretense of finding a bathroom. The town reminded her of Stoneridge, New Jersey, the small town where she'd been raised. They'd lunched at 'Jeremiah's Hole' and afterward, taken a short stroll along the waterfront. She recalled saying how pretty the town was and dreamt that one day they would settle down somewhere like it.

"You've got to be kidding!" John had said. "We'd both die of boredom out here. There isn't a theater or even a decent restaurant." At first, she'd been taken aback by his strong aversion to the town. They'd held such similar views in just about everything else, she'd assumed he would have liked the town as much as she. But then, she'd realized he'd always lived in large cities, so she shouldn't have been so surprised that he'd found Fenton too quiet.

Towards the end of 1997, she spotted an opportunity to revisit the prospect of moving to Fenton. John had proposed and they'd planned to marry the following July. At the time, their employer Smithfield Price, operated a strict security policy, citing that once married, couples were no longer allowed to work in the same department. As John was expected to make VP and she was just a personal assistant, it was natural to assume that she would make the sacrifice. However, instead of immediately acquiescing, she used the situation to leverage their move to Fenton. She told him that she had been there longer than he and she wasn't happy with any of the positions on offer. After an embarrassingly lengthy period in which John's boss started to question his commitment to the company, she told John she had come up with a solution. She would resign, providing that he agree to move to Fenton. So relieved to put an end to the matter, he conceded but only on the condition that they keep their apartment in the city. So just before Christmas of 1998, they moved into their house on Franklin. She hoped that John would eventually come to love Fenton as much as she.

Their house sat on top of a hill with a clear view of the Bay. She loved it, but sadly John failed to adjust to living there. His complaints were endless. But mostly he whined about the long commute, the heat in summer and how much work the old house needed. So that's why she'd decided to remodel, hoping to put an end to one of his complaints.

Sally opened the white wooden gate leading up to her house. Her spirits lifted when she saw the welcoming sight of the pink rose carpet before her. The petals fell silently, their perfume making her inhale deeply, involuntary. She closed her eyes and heard the sound of children's laughter from a memory buried deep inside. She was six. She and Ellie rolled about the lawn, throwing pink magnolia petals in the air.

"Your mom's not going to be happy when she sees the state of your dress, young lady," said her father.

"Shake the bushes daddy," she shouted, giggling uncontrollably.

She opened her eyes. The memory left her as quickly as it had appeared, leaving her feeling hollow. She let go of the gate and walked lightly over the rose petals to her front door. On entering the house, she was immediately hit by the sounds of music from a radio and sawing from the backyard.

The small square hallway was the main artery for the living room, dining room and kitchen areas. She closed the door behind her and walked straight ahead, then right, into her newly remodeled kitchen. She flipped the kettle on and chose a mug from one of the wall cupboards.

Her new kitchen consisted of light beech wood cabinets, black granite surfaces and stainless steel appliances. The wall between the kitchen and the living room had been removed and a breakfast bar was now in its place. On the other side of the bar, a small dining area with a table and four chairs and beyond that, another hallway leading to the three original bedrooms and a newly constructed one.

She spooned coffee into her mug, poured in the boiling water and gave it a sharp, quick stir. Intermittent banging came from the direction of the bedrooms, typifying the pace at which the remodel had progressed. The additional bedroom was constructed on the end of the original rear bedroom. The existing bedroom was now larger and so the outside wall had been removed. She had assumed that the new bedroom would be constructed before taking down the existing wall. But to Sally's horror, removing the original outer wall was the first thing the contractors did. Then the workmen didn't show for two weeks, resulting in that part of the house being exposed to the elements during the worst winter on record. Despite leaving several messages on her contractor's answering machine, it'd been a week before Joe had responded. Of course, he'd been full of apologies, saying that he'd had to pull his men off the job to help a client with an emergency plumbing problem. She'd bought it at first, but as time passed there had been numerous 'emergency jobs' the men had been called away to. Then materials wouldn't arrive, so the men walked off the job, saying they couldn't work without proper materials. And vice versa, deliveries would turn up, but the men wouldn't show. She quickly realized that her remodel was considered a fill-in job, something to do when there was nothing else for them to do. At first, she'd complained about it every week until eventually she turned to John for help. He went over the contract with her.

"You could certainly voice your disappointment about how slow the remodel is progressing, but legally you haven't got a leg to stand on." He threw the contract down on the breakfast table. "Really Sally, you should've discussed our expectations and had them written into the contract before signing it."

Our expectations! That's rich. He'd never taken any interest in the remodel from the start, she'd thought.

Realizing that the work would be completed at Joe's convenience, not hers, she somehow learned to live with it.

Shortly after discussing the contract with John, he started sleeping over at their apartment in the city, insisting that his workload had increased to such levels that it made no sense wasting precious time commuting during the week.

"Hi," said Andy, the carpenter. Known for his briskness, he was gone before she had time to return his greeting.

She picked up her coffee and followed him down the hallway.

"Hello, Mrs. Pringle," Matt said, passing her in the opposite direction.

"Hi," she answered.

The apprentice had joined McDouglas Construction fresh from high school. He wore a permanent frown, probably cultivated by the incessant teasing from Mike and Andy, the other two workmen. It seemed the more upset he became, the more they did it. Once fully qualified, she could well imagine Matt putting some other poor soul through the same kind of torture, like an abused, becoming an abuser.

She poked her head inside her old bedroom. Andy was on his knees fixing new doors to her closets. He was in his mid-thirties. His short, blonde hair was permanently coated with a thick layer of sawdust, making his piercing blue eyes all the more striking.

"Fuck! Fuck, fucking fuck!" she heard Mike yell from somewhere else in the house.

Andy shook his head and chuckled, but didn't turn around.

She found Mike in her new bathroom, his large, ungainly frame contorted into the small space beneath the washbasin. Although Joe had expressed confidence in Mike's ability to fit the bathroom, a twinge of apprehension ran through her at the unconvincing sight of a competent plumber. Joe had told her that Mike was a 'pain in the ass' but knew a thing or two about plumbing. She wondered if he had got around to using either of these two things yet.

"Hi," Mike mumbled through the cigarette drooping from the corner of his mouth. He pried himself from under the sink. Still on his knees, he rummaged through his toolbox. He had on the same black, grimy trousers he always wore. They hung below a flabby stomach and bagged from behind making his bottom look deflated. If he put them on back to front they would probably have fitted better. Covering his top half, he wore a black, washed out vest baring numerous holes.

It was hard to tell how old Mike was because he wore a permanent hung-over expression. His hair was a dark, greasy matted mess, which didn't look as though it had seen a comb in years. He drove an old, white rusty pickup truck, littered with empty beer cans. It was guarded by a Great Dane, called Scotty, who despite Sally's endless protests, used her backyard as a toilet. Mike bragged that he knew just about everyone in town, she suspected it was the other way around. He picked up a hammer and returned to his tortuous position under the washbasin.

"Ouch, bastard!" he yelled, dropping the hammer to comfort a finger.

"Phone's ringing, Mrs. Pringle!" Matt shouted.

"Thanks!" Sally rushed back through the house to the kitchen, thinking that a wrench was more befitting pipe connection than a hammer.

She picked up the receiver. "Hello?"

"Hello Sally, it's mom."

"Mother! Oh, how are you?" Having never seen eye-to-eye, she sat down on the kitchen stool, and prepared to listen hard, knowing that her mother communicated as much with what she didn't say, than with what she did.

"I'm fine. I've called because I've been doing a lot of thinking lately and, well, we never really see much of each other anymore, do we? I know I've only myself to blame. I've been so preoccupied with business I've neglected spending time with the people that mean most to me. So, I was thinking … Well, how would you feel if I came to stay for a few days, maybe a week?"

"Oh!"

"I thought we could go shopping together and you know, hang out."

Hang out. What on earth does she mean? "Well, yes, mom that would be great. But have you forgotten that we're in the middle of a remodel?" She turned to look in the direction of the banging, hoping her mother could hear it over the phone. "You know you haven't exactly picked the best time to visit!" she snapped.

She didn't want her mother to come. She would criticize, Sally would get upset, and then there would be the most awful row, followed by silence that would last for months. That was how it had gone in the past and she was glad they didn't do it anymore. It had been more than a couple of years since they had seen each other and Sally was quite happy with the occasional phone call.

From Sally's point of view the conflict between them started in her teens. As the owner of a large development corporation, her mother worked twenty-four, seven. Sally's father, considering himself an inventor, spent most of his day tinkering around the tool shed and so by default became her 'go to' parent. However, it was her mother who'd constantly lecture her about schoolwork and yell at her when she received notes from teachers complaining about her grades.

"Sally, school's so important," she would say. "Don't you care about your future? Don't you think it would be a shame not to be able to go to university, because you didn't apply yourself at school?"

"But you didn't mom! Did you! You were given it on a plate! How can you lecture me about school!" she would

31

snap back. As far as she was concerned her mother had never treated her well, and was never around when she needed her. The last straw was her mother's disapproval of John. She had been gracious enough to attend their wedding, but they had not seen each other since. So Sally was extremely suspicious by this sudden interest to reconnect. But finding no more excuses and unable to bear the silence any longer, she relented. "Well why not, yes it would be lovely. When were you thinking of?"

"Well, there's a 11:00 am flight tomorrow."

"Tomorrow!" she bellowed. "Mom how about next week? Maybe I could persuade John to take some time off work?" She knew full well that he wouldn't, especially for her mom, she was just playing for time. *Damn! I won't have the opportunity to cancel!*

"No, that won't work. I'm having my second round of chemo next week. I'm usually exhausted for about a week after that …"

Trust her to use her illness to get her own way. About eight months ago, her mother told her she'd developed ovarian cancer. She'd spared her the details and Sally was only too happy to be kept in the dark. To contemplate her mother's demise would expose her to the sack full of emotions she'd managed to keep at bay. Whenever she scratched the surface, she felt guilty and severely resented it.

"Then tomorrow would be fine," Sally said, finally realizing that she was left with no room to maneuver.

"Great! Then I'll see you tomorrow. I'll get a taxi from the airport, so don't worry about …"

Sally wasn't listening anymore. She was wondering what they could possibly do together.

"… Around dinnertime."

"Okay mom, see you tomorrow."

"Looking forward to it. Bye dear."

Dazed, she replaced the receiver, wondering how she was going to survive the week. Drifting through the house, she entered her old bedroom, forgetting that Andy was in there. She turned to leave.

"What do you think?" Andy asked, stopping her in her tracks. He nodded towards the closet doors.

"Oh great, they're really nice," she said indifferently. *I don't even know what she likes to do?*

He got up from the floor, grabbed a water bottle from the dresser and drank thirstily from it.

John's going to have a fit when she turns up.

"I had to custom make the doors," he said, wiping his mouth on the back of his sleeve. "The regular size…"

"What?"

"The doors. I had to custom make the doors," he explained.

"Oh right. That figures," she replied. *Maybe we could go away together for a few days. Up to Napa. Keep her out of John's way.*

Andy took off his baseball cap and smoothed back his hair sending dust into the air.

"Yeah. That's how it goes," he said. "Say, who's the guy in the photo," he asked, pointing with the bottle to a photograph on the dresser.

"My father. He, my father, used to be good at carpentry."

"Oh yeah?"

33

"He made me a doll's house once." She flushed suddenly realizing how stupid she had made him sound. "But he was an inventor. He worked with a variety of different materials."

"And your mom? I don't see a photo of your mom."

That's none of your dammed business! She glared out of the window. Guilt and anger suddenly percolated inside her. She felt him staring at her.

"I'm sorry, I didn't mean to pry." He knelt down and returned his attention to the closet doors. "It's just in a job like this, you can't help but notice the stuff people have in their homes. You know photos, personal stuff. And before you know it, you've formed an opinion of them. Then, when you move to the next job you wonder whether you got it right?"

He bent over, picked up a screw from the floor and slotted it into a hinge.

She took a deep breath and swiftly blinked away some tears that had formed.

"I never see them again, so it shouldn't really matter," he continued. "Seems unfair to paint the wrong picture though, don't you think?"

She didn't answer.

"People do it all the time." He pulled a screwdriver from his tool belt and screwed the hinge to the door.

Sally drifted to the bedroom door. "She's coming tomorrow."

Andy turned to face her. "Who?"

"My mother," she said. "She's coming tomorrow."

Oh!" He turned back to his work. "That's nice."

34

Tony Mitchell stood in front of his mother's gravestone 'Alyssa Mitchell nee Lubian, Native of Greece,' it read. A gust of wind blew some leaves over it. He glanced at the sky. Clouds massed into dark, threatening depressions, making the sky look gloomier by the second.

He pulled out an old, creased photograph from his wallet. Tears stung his eyes as he looked down at the image of his mother as a child with the family she had left behind in Greece, some 60 years ago. She couldn't have been more than 12 years old in the photograph. He'd found it in a shoebox amongst the letters and postcards he had sorted through the day after her funeral. On the back were the names of the people in the shot. The other two children, Mikolas and Egidio, he assumed were his mother's brothers, his uncles. She never spoke of her family, or her early life in Greece. And on the few occasions he had asked, she had replied curtly, "Why speak of the past. It is wasteful!" As she had been such a small, fragile woman, he had assumed that he'd inherited his powerful upper body from his English father. But now he could clearly see the same wide chest and strong shoulders on his uncles.

His father had abandoned them in the US when he was two and he had never met any of his extended family from either side. They'd just been his mom, himself and Mr. Englestein, a Jewish librarian who had been a lifelong tenant and companion of his mother's. It was Englestein who convinced him as a teen, to leave gang life behind, and start over somewhere new. Having little in terms of education, and a rising rap sheet, he decided to follow his father's footsteps into the British Army. The military had taken most of his life and now he bitterly regretted not spending more time with his mother. *And now she's gone.* He sucked in his breath and exhaled, with a sigh. The photograph was all he had left. A drop of rain fell onto the image. He wiped the photograph on his shirt, slipped it back into his wallet, and returned the wallet into the inside top pocket of his black leather jacket.

A flutter of wings made him look up. A pigeon had landed on the outstretched hand of the angel statue on his mother's headstone. It cooed and cocked its head from side to side. He followed its motion, entranced. Always open to the mysteries of the universe, he wondered whether the bird was a messenger from the other side and whether it sensed his pain. It caught Tony's eye and stopped cooing, and then with his full attention, defecated on his mother's gravestone.

"Bastard!" he yelled. The bird flew off, but it didn't get far. Tony promptly took out his revolver and shot it. The bird fell to the ground with a dull thud.

He strutted down the hill to his dark blue Audi, parked by the curbside. After rounding the back of the car, he caught a glimpse of himself in the driver's door mirror, stopping him in his tracks. *Who the hell am I?* He'd had so many disguises and identities over the years, he didn't know who he was anymore. "For fucks sake," he said, yanking the driver's door open. *Get a grip!* Once inside, he picked up his phone and dialed.

"Tonight!" he said. He threw the phone onto the passenger seat, turned the ignition and drove sharply away.

4

At precisely 8:55 pm dressed in night combat gear, Tony ran furtively along the back of the fence to the gap he'd conveniently found the night before. He dropped his kitbag, bent over and peered through it. *Yes! Like clockwork.* As usual, there she sat, by the lampshade, reading a book and sipping a glass of white wine.

He knelt down, unzipped his bag and swiftly plucked out his rifle. The Ruger 77/22 Hornet was not his usual choice of weapon but then again this wasn't his usual kind of job. Espionage, assassination and kidnapping of prominent officials, legitimate or otherwise, was his game. He took on jobs others wouldn't. And when others fucked up, 'the fixer' as he was known, would be called in to finish the job. He was expensive but he was the best.

"Make it look as unprofessional as possible. Our client doesn't want it to look like a hit," Leung had said.

"A hit's a hit, pal. You want it done or not?"

"Up to you." Leung had shrugged his shoulders. "$300,000 cash. Easy money. Easy money. And … then we even."

Tony needed the money because he couldn't touch his bank account. The US had been leaning on the Swiss authorities to monitor transactions between their banks for the last three months. They were probably after drug money, but all the same, he didn't want their attention. And now he was short of cash and Leung's offer had been too good to turn down.

But a hit on home turf was totally different to a hit overseas. Typically, assassinations came with a fully completed reconnaissance report detailing his victim's routine, a readily supply of equipment, and a backup crew he trusted, should things go belly up. All he had to do was work out the time, location and method, then do the business; he was usually in and out within a couple of hours. His only rule was not to take on high profile hits on home territory, best not to "shit in one's own backyard" as it were. Since this job was neither high profile nor prestigious, he had to work independently and do all the leg work himself. Instead of a few hours, it could take anything from a few days to a couple of weeks. So, by its very nature, this kind of job exposed him to a higher probability of detection and as such, was a much riskier proposition. On top of that, as with this case, it was harder to plan a hit on a target with no set schedule. Her only routine was her early morning run. So, he figured, this would have be the time and the place.

That left the question of method; what weapon to use. When contracted to make a victim look like they had died of natural causes, an injection of Ricin was a no brainer. At the very most, the victim would notice nothing more than a strange looking pinprick on their skin. Symptoms mimic stomach flu but death inevitably follows within a couple of days. However, his attempt at injecting his target with Ricin the day before had been aborted at the very last moment. For some reason, she had started her run later than usual, resulting in them crossing paths, not in the wilderness part of the trail as planned, but closer to town, and at a location with too many potential witnesses. It had been a split second decision, but the right one. And now he was pleased that he had taken time to prepare for plan B.

Along with the rifle that Leung had supplied him, he had purchased a BB gun and had spent the past few weeks using both weapons to shoot out windows in the neighborhood. His plan was to make the shootings appear amateurish. It wasn't exactly the most sophisticated cover but he was short on time and irritated by the caliber of the job. He knew Leung didn't really care a shit about the cover, but being Chinese, reputation was everything, so he had to make some sort of effort. But he hoped the cheeky bugger didn't tell anyone that he had done the job. Tony also had a reputation to keep and he would never live this down, should his peers find out about it.

He poked the Ruger 77/22 Hornet through the fence. Leung was on the money, the .22 Hornet's higher velocity, made it effective for the job but anybody finding a spent round would assume it came from the much less powerful .22lr 'varminter' that kids shot at rodents, cans and stop signs.

But for a hit, it presented a challenge. To do any significant damage to a human using this weapon, one would have to hit soft, vulnerable areas of the body. For a kill shot, the eye socket at a firing range of "too bloody close for comfort," was pretty much the only option. It was going to take a steady hand from a static position. It was so light, even breathing made the scope vibrate and his victim was no clearer than a quivering blur of beige and blue. But what Tony lacked in hardware, he could make up with his mind and body, a concept he'd been introduced to during his training with the Special Boat Services, an elite division of the British Military. His free diving skills had prepared him for much harder jobs than this. At his peak, he could hold his breath for four minutes and decrease his heart rate to 30 beats per minute. So this should be a breeze.

Mustering all his powers of concentration, he slowed his breathing and decreased his heartbeat, until he eventually stopped breathing altogether. As his focus sharpened, he caught sight of the title of the book she was reading, 'Perfect Relationships,' by Dr. A. H. Purdue. *There's irony for you,* he thought. He moved his scope up to his victim's head and focused on her right eye. His finger tightened around the trigger, just as an unprecedented sensation entered his consciousness. His nose itched. Then it ran. Concentration lost, he started panting. He pulled away, and irately wiped his nose on his sleeve. The delay made him edgy and that haunting feeling surfaced again. He was losing his touch.

With clear nasal passages, he realized the cause of his irritation, creosote from the fence. He quickly repositioned himself and once more centered his target. Again, after using

41

his meditative skills, he clearly focused his victim and increased pressure on the trigger. Suddenly his target jumped up from her seat and walked out of view. *Shit! Shit! Shit!*

He pulled the rifle away, fell back against the fence and breathed. He felt dizzy, as the blood returned to his arteries at warp speed. Damp, cold sweat pitted his brow. Rummaging through his pocket, he pulled out a handkerchief and blew fiercely into it, relieving both his nose and his frustration. He reproached himself for being suckered into the job in the first place and for not handling his finances better. He should have diversified, put some of his money into the Channel Islands. Anything to avoid the position he now found himself in.

But mostly, he was annoyed by the nature of the job. He didn't know for sure, but this was probably a domestic and domestics were not his thing. He usually avoided them like the plague, believing them to be well below his expertise and therefore deleterious to his reputation. And, in truth, he had little respect for the man on the street. By and large, he thought they were petty, greedy and small minded, and he could not understand why people in western societies would resort to violence. He'd spent a great deal of time working in the nastier parts of the world and had seen it all; drug lords, sex traders, real scum of the earth. People in the West, with their boring little lives, didn't know how lucky they were. It irritated him to think that anyone would resort to having their spouse murdered, rather than finding a way to make their marriage work.

Tony considered junking the job altogether, catching an earlier flight to London, and his connection to Athens. But then again, the extra $300,000 would come in handy and he was indebted to Leung. A few months ago, at short notice, his Chinese friend had miraculously managed to smuggle some specialized bomb making equipment to him in Belize. He owed him big time. And lastly, more importantly, there was pride. Leung was sure to make it known he'd fucked up.

Tony surveyed the entire house and noticed a room lit at the opposite end. *'Number one rule. Never deviate from a plan once initiated, unless absolutely necessary,'* echoed Sergeant Jones' words. Old habits die hard. Odds were, she'd return to her reading.

Waiting patiently, Tony rested against the fence with his arms folded across his chest, checking every minute or so to see if she had returned. Dew from the grass, seeped into his pants. His watch read 9:15 pm. Driven by boredom and curiosity, he went over to the other end of the fence to see if he could spot her. However, there were no cracks or holes in the fence and therefore no way to see.

Tony paced the ground debating his options. *This isn't looking good. If she doesn't return to the living room soon, she'll probably head straight to bed and I'll have to put the hit off until tomorrow night - fuck!* His foot hit against something hard. He squatted and felt around his feet. Several pieces of broken concrete were scattered around the ground. He picked up a couple of the larger pieces and stacked them up against the fence. Then he stepped on them and had just enough height to peer over. There she was, staring out of the window.

Fuck it, bugger protocol. He gave the fence a quick shake, then went to retrieve his rifle.

After rechecking that she was still there, Tony threw his rifle over the fence. He grabbed the fence on both sides of a supporting post and jumped up, locking his arms. But the fence moaned under his weight, then peeled away beneath him. He fell down clasping the top half of the fence, smashing his genitals against the supporting post as he fell. He hit the ground hard and noisily, planting his face firmly in the earth. Tony groaned with pain. He would have comforted his trouser tackle but for the fact that his fingers were trapped beneath the fence. An overwhelming odor hit his nostrils. *Shit! Fuck! It's shit!* Adjusting his weight, he freed his hands, curled into a ball, and gave his genitals the overdue attention they deserved.

Still holding his privates, Tony rolled onto his side. His target was pressed up against the window, her hands cupped over her brow, straining to see out. She'd obviously heard the commotion but he knew he was too far out to be spotted. She, on the other hand, was in perfect view. Frantically, he felt around for his rifle, not caring what he put his hands on. What could be worse than a face full of dog shit? Eventually, his fingertips tapped his gun and he quickly drew it to him.

His attention moved from the pain between his legs, to the upper part of his body, as he concentrated once more on his target. Yet again, he felt the tingling sensation in his nostrils, but ignored it, fearing that at any moment she would move from the window and the opportunity be missed. He lifted himself onto his elbows, braced the gun on his shoulder and peered through the scope. Aiming was a breeze now that he was closer.

44

Stay there love, stay there. Slowly he tightened his finger on the trigger. At the exact moment he fired, he sneezed. The window shattered, but Tony knew he had missed.

Sally screamed and dropped to the floor, staring incredulously at the shattered window. *What the hell was that?* A shard of glass fell from her hair. Panting, she scanned the floor searching amongst the fragments for a rock or some similar missile.

She glanced around the bare room and noticed a tiny mark on the opposite wall to the window. Terror overtook her as she realized what it was. "Oh God, oh God!" she whimpered. Frantically, she scrambled on all fours across the floor, her arms so pumped with adrenalin, she was through the door in seconds.

She paused at the other end of the hallway, looking longingly at the front door. It was temptingly close but in direct view of the back patio door, exposing her to whoever was outside.

"Oh ... oh ...", she whimpered. She shook. "Think ... think," she willed herself. Sally glanced at the telephone on the kitchen counter. *The bedroom.* She spun around and crawled into her old bedroom. Her arms shook, but she managed to keep them moving, smashing the bedroom door into the wall. The room was unlit, but she was at the telephone before the door swung back and plunged the room into darkness. She snatched the mobile hand piece

45

from the phone base and rapidly crawled to the other side of the bed, away from the door. Her breathing saturated any other sound to her ears. She sat up against the bed, cursing that the old phone didn't have a backlight. She tried feeling her way over the numbers. "The number you've dialed is unavailable," said a voice. She dropped the phone and cried with fear and frustration. Noticing a patch of light on the floor, illuminated by a street lamp through the window, she picked up the phone again and scrambled over to the shaft of light. She held the phone in the light's path and with a shaking forefinger dialed 911.

"Police, or fire?" said a woman.

"Pla ..," Pla ... Police," she gasped. Police! Gunz. Someone's fired a gun. Help! Please help!"

"OK, OK ma'am, we're locating your address now," the dispatcher said.

She heard a creak from a floorboard outside the bedroom. Terrified that the shooter was coming for her, she looked for a place to hide.

"Ma'am, are you still there?"

Her breaths were so shallow, she couldn't reply. Buzzing filled her ears. She could barely hear the dispatcher, who sounded distant, as though she were speaking from the other end of a long, narrow tunnel. She stopped shaking but couldn't feel the phone in her hand anymore. She realized that she was about to pass out. "Ma'am! Ma'am," the dispatcher demanded.

Sally moaned into the mouthpiece. She forced a couple of long, deep breaths into her body. Feeling a rapid rush of blood to her head, she suddenly became cognizant again.

46

But not wanting an intruder to hear where she was, Sally didn't answer the dispatcher's relentless banter. Deciding the closets were the best place to hide, she crawled towards them still holding the telephone. "Ma'am! Ma'am!" the dispatcher continued shouting. Damp with perspiration, she opened the closet door, crawled inside and closed it after her. With her back against the closet wall, she held the phone tight against one ear and tried to listen to the sounds in the house with the other.

"Ma'am!"

"Yes. I'm here," Sally whispered.

"You're at 23 Franklin? Is that correct?"

"Yes. Please help me."

"What's your name ma'am?"

"S … Sally. Sally Pringle."

"Sally. Try to stay calm. There's a patrol car on the way. Don't hang up. Stay on the line. Sally, who fired the gun?"

"I don't know!" she snapped. "Someone shot at me through the window!"

"Can you see or hear anything now?"

Sally listened intently.

"Sally, are you still there? Sally?"

"Yes, I'm still here! Where the hell do you think I am!"

"It's important to stay calm," the dispatcher said evenly. "Can you hear anything?"

"Shut up, I'm trying to listen and the only dammed thing I can hear is you. And will you please stop telling me to calm down!"

Finally, the dispatcher fell silent. Sally heard another creak. *Was that from the living room, or the hallway? Was it a footstep or just the house?* She visualized a man dressed in black, creeping nearer, finding his way to her. She was on the brink of losing it. The urge to run through the house was great.

Then she heard a screech of tires outside.

"Sally, the police are at your front door. Can you get to the door?"

"Oh, thank God, yes, I think so."

"But don't hang up. Put the receiver down and get to the front door."

She placed the receiver on the floor without making a sound. Slowly, she pushed open the closet door and scanned the bedroom. Praying that the noises she heard were either the creation of her imagination or the house settling for the night, she crept from the closet and crawled along the floor to the bedroom door. She held her breath as she gently pulled it open. The house was eerily silent. The only sound was the steady buzz of the refrigerator. She sighed with relief. Poking her head into the hallway, she glanced in both directions. The coast was clear. The floorboards in front of her suddenly creaked, making her flinch and suck in her breath. It was nothing, just her weight, flexing the floor.

She wiped the sweat from her brow and crawled down the hallway into the living room, scanning as she went. The sound of the refrigerator grew menacingly louder. She contemplated her next move. If she made a dash to the door from where she was, she'd be fully exposed to the outside by the back patio door. Realizing that the couch would give her the best cover, she briskly crawled across the living room floor to the near end of the couch and then along its back to the other end. She poked her head out, glancing once at the patio door and then made a dash for the front door.

Sally pulled at the door, but it was dead bolted. Her heart raced as she fumbled to unlock it. Finally, she yanked it open. A policeman stood there pointing his gun at her. Instinctively, she held up her hands as if to surrender. He unceremoniously grabbed her arm and pushed her toward the street. "Go! Go! Go!" he yelled.

She ran down the path towards a patrol car. A female police officer pointing a gun in her direction, stood up from behind the open driver's door. Without taking her eyes off the house, the officer sidestepped to the back of the car, and with her free hand opened the back door.

"In here," the officer ordered. Sally quickly jumped into the backseat. The door slammed behind her and the officer promptly returned to her crouching position behind the driver's door.

Panting, Sally looked back at the house. She heard voices from across the street. A dozen or so neighbors had gathered on the sidewalk. She could hear the faint sounds of police sirens in the distance. Wet with perspiration, she wiped her face with the bottom of her t-shirt. The sirens grew menacingly louder. Then two police patrol cars, lights ablaze, burst through the darkness at the end of the street, skidding to a halt in front of her. A couple of uniformed cops leapt from the first car, followed by two plainclothes men from the one behind. They ran to either side of her house, their guns drawn.

"Get back," shouted the woman police officer, to the people who had crept near the car. The crowd stopped moving but didn't back away.

The police officer who had first come to her rescue, came out of her house. The female police officer straightened from her position, slammed the door shut and met him on the drive. A larger crowd had now gathered on the street and the car was now surrounded. Some stared inside at Sally. She felt like an exhibit at a zoo. Dan Spetzen, one of her neighbors was in his pajamas and bathrobe. She heard him say something about, "Kids again!" and "The Tribune," to another neighbor.

Of course! That's it! It was a BB gun. Another one of those student pranks. Sally slumped back into the seat, closing her eyes with relief. A knock on the window made her jump. Dan's face was pressed against the window. He shouted something to her but she couldn't hear. The patrol car had no handles to open the door nor to wind down the window.

"I can't hear," she shouted, pointing to her ear.

"Are you OK?" Dan yelled.

"Yes. Just a bit shaken!"

"Those kids need sorting out. Scaring the life outta folks like that. They're gonna give someone a heart attack before long!" he yelled.

Sally smiled weakly at him. The female police officer came to the roadside of the car. "OK, OK, show's over folks. Go home!"

Dan and the other bystanders backed away from the car.

The door nearest the curb suddenly opened.

"Mrs. Pringle? Detective Darnell, Solano County Sheriff's Department." He was a large built man about 50, with a buzz cut and a reddish complexion. He held his badge in front of her face. "You OK? Are you hurt?" He replaced his badge inside his jacket pocket.

"I'm fine, just a bit shaken. Did you catch anyone?"

"No, but we're still working on it. Were you alone tonight?"

"Yes, my husband's in San Francisco."

"You might want to call him," he advised. "Tell him to come home."

"But if it's just a kid's prank," she said, smiling. "I really don't think it's necessary to bother him."

"Mrs. Pringle, you should call him." Darnell said firmly.

She studied his face. He seemed serious. "You mean, oh God. You mean, someone actually tried to shoot me?" she asked.

"Now, best not to jump to conclusions. Ballistics and forensics aren't here yet," he explained. "And until we've fully investigated, it's difficult to know what we have here."

What's he saying? That I should be worried, or shouldn't?

"But I need to take a statement from you."

"Yes, of course."

He straightened, held the door wider and stood back in order for her to exit the car. For a moment Sally didn't move. *A real bullet! Someone really tried to shoot me?*

"Mrs. Pringle," Darnell said, peering into the car.

Shaken, she slowly got out of the car. A police van had appeared from somewhere. Two uniformed police officers with dogs, stood in front of it talking to one of the plainclothes officers. A white van suddenly careened around the corner, dispersing the crowd as it made its way down the street, finally stopping in the middle of the road, beside the patrol car. A woman with a microphone followed by a cameraman jumped from it and pushed through the crowd in Sally's direction. They were intercepted by the female police officer, who blocked their path.

"Mrs. Pringle, Channel 11 news!" the woman shouted. "Who do you think did this? Detective Darnell, can you give us a statement?"

"Get back," ordered the police officer. The newswoman tried to push the microphone over the officer's head toward them. "I'm warning you, move back," the officer repeated.

Darnell ignored the reporter and opened his arm, guiding Sally toward the house and away from the newswoman. She felt swamped by his size. Another officer was placing yellow caution tape around her front garden. She glanced at Darnell for an explanation. He offered none.

She stepped inside her house. It seemed strangely hollow and distant, like she was visiting a previously owned home. The police were everywhere, outside in the backyard, in the kitchen, dashing in and out of the hallway to the rear bedrooms, like an infestation.

An officer approached Darnell, and whispered something into the detective's ear.

"Excuse me a moment." He left Sally's side and stepped away to talk privately with the officer.

She tried to internalize the scene before her. Chilled by the temperature and by the sight of the police rushing around, she rubbed her arms.

"Mrs. Pringle," Darnell shouted over to her. "This might be a good time for you to call your husband."

"Oh, OK," she said.

Darnell and the officer immediately returned to their conversation. She strolled over to the telephone and picked up the receiver. Her hand shook as she remembered her frantic call to 911.

She pressed the speed dial button to their apartment in the city. It rang several times before the recording cut in. "Hello, you have reached, ..." said John's voice. Sally felt totally alone. *This might not have happened if he'd been here. Why couldn't he be like Frank or Eric? They came home every night.* "... leave a message after the tone."

"John ... John, it's Sally. Something's happened. Someone's tried to ... well ... someone's shot at the house. I'm scared John, please come home." Then she called his cell phone, again it went to messaging, so she left a similar message.

"Mrs. Pringle!" Darnell was now standing in the living room area.

She combed her fingers through her limp hair and went over to join him. He pulled out a notepad and pen from the inside pocket of his suit jacket as they both sat down. "Did you manage to get hold of your husband?"

"No, he's probably turned off his cell phone to work. I've left him messages." She glanced over her shoulder, intimidated by the frenzied activity around her.

He checked his watch, opened his notepad and scribbled something in it. "OK, Mrs. Pringle, what happened tonight?"

"Well, I was reading and the telephone rang," she glanced over her shoulder to the phone on the kitchen counter.

"Approximately what time was that?"

"About 9:00 o'clock. Yes, it was 9:00 pm."

"Where were you when the phone rang?" He asked.

"Here, I was sitting where you are."

He glanced at the empty wine glass on the small side table. "What makes you so sure about the time?"

"I always read with a glass of wine about that time every night. It's a habit of mine." She felt her face heat up as she realized how that must have sounded.

He made another note in his notepad. She hoped that he hadn't got the impression she'd been drunk, although she could do with a stiff drink now.

"Who was on the phone?" he asked.

"John, my husband."

"What did he say?" Darnell shifted in his seat but kept his head down.

"He told me he would be staying overnight in the city."

He looked up surprised. "Does he often stay in the city at night?"

"Oh no," she said smiling, thinking the detective had got the impression that he was spending a night on the town. "John works there. We own an apartment on Taylor, on Nob Hill. He's been working long hours lately. It just makes more sense for him to stay in the city during the week."

Darnell nodded but stared intensely at her.

She shifted her weight, coughed nervously into her fist, then faced the floor.

"Who does he work for?" he asked.

54

"Smithfield Price. Investment Bankers on Montgomery."

"How long has he worked there?"

"About 11 years," she said, frowning at him. *What's this got to do with the shooting?*

"Would you say your husband's good at his job?"

"Why, yes!"

"Has he had any problems at work lately?"

"No!" she replied.

"What else did he say?"

"Just small talk," she snapped, irritated by his line of questioning. "He said that he'd had a hard day. General chitchat about work. But, what's this got to do with the shooting?"

"Just procedure, Mrs. Pringle," Darnell replied coolly. "Did he sound his usual self?"

"Yes! Why shouldn't he?" she snapped.

"OK, now what happened after the phone call?"

"Well, I went into the new bedroom, at the back of the house," she replied sharply, still frazzled by his questioning.

"What for?" he asked.

"What?"

"Why did you go to the bedroom?"

"I don't know! I just did!" *For God's sake, can't we just move on to what happened?* She remembered feeling disappointed when John told her he was not coming home. She said she understood and pleaded with him not to work all night, as he was often too tired to do anything with her at the weekend. This was not unusual, but this time she felt abandoned and pondered whether the personal sacrifices he was making for his career were damaging their relationship. But she wasn't going to tell Darnell that.

Darnell's eyes penetrated her. She felt that he could see straight through her. She glanced at the chaos around her, trying to detach herself from the detective's intense scrutiny.

"OK, so you went to the back bedroom. How long were you there?" he asked, making more notes.

"Oh five, ten minutes, maybe a little longer, I don't remember. It was probably less than fifteen minutes."

"What did you do in there?"

"Nothing."

He looked up from his notepad. "Nothing?"

"Thinking,"

"Thinking? Thinking about what?" he asked.

"Look, is this really necessary! I mean is what I was thinking going to catch whoever did this!"

One of Darnell's eyebrows rose, and again he made notes.

She felt like a criminal. She wanted to snatch the notepad from his hands and tear it to pieces. *God damm it, I'm the victim here!*

"OK, what happened next?"

"I heard a noise!" she said tersely. "From outside!"

"What kind of noise?"

"A crashing sound, like something falling. I thought that maybe the sunshade had blown over in the wind. So I went to the window, but I couldn't see anything. It was too dark. Then it happened."

"The shot?" he asked.

"Yes."

She tried to recall whether she'd heard the shot before the window had smashed. She imagined the bullet slowly torpedoing through the window, hitting her through the head and spewing blood all over the room as she was propelled backward onto the floor. She shuddered.

"Go on," Darnell said.

"I dropped to the floor, crawled into my old bedroom, and called 911."

"Did you hear anything else from outside?"

"No, that's it."

A police officer came over and whispered into the detective's ear.

"Excuse me, a moment, would you?" Darnell got up and followed the officer to the hallway where they huddled in conversation.

Sally watched the commotion around her. She couldn't tell how many people there were because they moved around so quickly. Two cops with the words 'Forensics' on the back of their jackets walked in through the front door and straight out through the back. She felt lightheaded, detached, as though if she reached out she'd touch a movie screen.

Darnell returned to Sally's side. "Do you have a friend or a neighbor you could stay with until your husband gets here?"

"Uh, yes, Helen Pearce. She's lives on High Bank."

"Bruin!" he shouted.

The female police officer appeared from the backyard.

"Mary. Take Mrs. Pringle to her friend's house would you? I'm done for now," he said to Sally. "But I'll need to go over a few more details in the morning." He turned in the direction of the backyard.

"But what about John? I left a message for him to come home. He'll wonder where I am."

"That's OK. We need to ask him a few questions anyway. We'll let him know where you are."

She glanced between the two officers. "Questions? What sort of questions? Why do you want to question John?"

"Police procedure ma'am. Just doing my job," Darnell said, quickly disappearing through the patio door.

"What's your friend's name and telephone number?" Mary asked.

Sally combed her hand through her hair. "Helen, Helen Pearce, two six two, five seven four two."

"Why don't you go and put together an overnight bag and I'll let your friend know your coming."

Sally slowly walked into the bedroom hallway. The door to the new addition was open. A couple of officers were in there, talking and taking photographs. She stared at the broken window. One of the cops followed her line of sight.

"We're just about done here," he said. "You can call a window repairer now if you want."

She nodded and walked into her old bedroom.

5

At approximately 10:15 pm Sally and Mary, the police officer, pulled onto the Pearce's drive. By the time they'd climbed out of the patrol car, her friends were standing by their front door. Helen was in her dressing gown. Frank was still wearing daytime clothes. Carrying her overnight bag, Sally walked wearily towards them. Her body ached, her muscles tight with adrenaline.

Helen came rushing down the drive. "Are you OK?"

Sally nodded yes, but felt far from OK.

Helen placed a comforting arm around her, guiding her towards the house, as if she were some old, frail woman. When they caught up to Frank, he kindly relieved her of her bag.

Inside, Sally's attention was drawn to the TV bellowing out an advert for laser eye surgery. The image of a woman suddenly being able to see clearly, was prophetic; being blindsided by the shootings and her recent realization that she and John were drifting apart.

"Come on, sit down," Helen said.

Still mesmerized by the advert, Sally was steered to the couch. She took off her black fleece jacket and laid it across the coffee table.

Frank closed the front door after Mary had entered and immediately struck up a conversation with her.

"Can I get you anything Sally?" Helen asked. "A drink? Something to eat?"

"I'm not hungry, but a glass of water would be great. Thank you."

Helen disappeared into the kitchen and Sally dropped onto the couch. She kicked off her shoes and gave her feet a quick massage. Her neck ached. She closed her eyes and rolled her head a few times.

Tuning into Mary and Frank's conversation, she heard Mary say that someone had shot at the house and that Sally was still a bit shaken. Sally glanced over at the two. Mary said that John would be informed of Sally's whereabouts as soon as he had been contacted.

Mary stood with her hands on her hips. She wore her light, blonde hair tied in a bun at the nape of her neck. Her full, curvy figure seemed constricted in her police uniform. Frank listened with one hand in his trouser pocket while the other stroked his chin. His gray streaked hair lay flat against one side of his head, as though he'd been lying down for some time. Sally noted that he had put on some weight, his waistband disappeared under his stomach. She reflected on how different he was from John, both physically and in personality. John was tall and thin, while Frank was about 5'8", rotund, and much fleshier. Although he had been a computer programmer for as long as computers had been

60

around, he'd refused promotion several times, preferring the easy life to the added pressures of management. In contrast, John was driven by promotion. When they met for dinner, Frank had little conversation other than news about the latest computer technology, often drifting away from the dinner table to read a fishing magazine. More than a few times, she wondered what Helen saw in him. He seemed too much of a contrast to her bubbly, outgoing personality and too unkempt for her fastidiousness. Though, recently, she complained that they were in a rut, that Frank was unwilling to try new things. "All he wants to do is sit in front of the TV with a beer at night. It's as though he's dying to get old."

Sally heard Mary say John's name.

"… is on his way from the city. We've told Mrs. Pringle that we'll let him know …"

"Here you are." Helen had returned from the kitchen with Sally's water and sat down beside her.

"I'm so sorry about this Helen. You look as though you were ready for bed."

"Don't be silly. You know we are always here for you," she said. "What happened?"

"I was in the back bedroom, when I heard a noise from the garden. I thought maybe the wind had blown something over, but when I looked through the window I couldn't see anything. Then the window shattered." Sally sipped some of her water. "There was glass everywhere, in my hair, my clothes. I searched the floor for a rock or something. Then I spotted a hole in the wall. Next minute I know, I'm on all fours racing out of the room." She shivered recalling the terrifying moment.

"It must have been awful," Helen said. "This must be the fourth in two weeks. It's about time the police caught whoever's doing this."

Sally was a little taken aback by her friend's composure. *Of course, she must think that it was a BB gun.* She placed her glass on the table and turned to her. "Helen, the police haven't said yet but I don't think it was a BB gun. It was a real bullet."

"My God, Sally! And you were at the window? You're lucky to be alive!"

"Helen. Why would someone want to harm us?" She started tearing up.

"Oh, come on. That's crazy." She placed an arm around Sally's shoulder. "Anybody, even kids nowadays, can get their hands on guns. This could have happened to anyone. Why, we only live a few blocks away!"

"Yes, I guess you're right."

Mary came over and squatted in front of Sally. "I'm going now. If you need me, call. Here's my number." She wrote on the back of a card and slipped it into her hand. Sally noted her wide, green eyes and enviable complexion. Mary patted her arm, then stood up. "And try to get a good night's sleep. I'll see you in the morning."

Frank escorted Mary to the door and showed her out. The telephone rang. "I'll get it," he said, rushing to the bureau. "Yes, yes, she is, just a second ...Sally, it's John."

Sally leapt from the couch and snatched the receiver from him. "Thank god! Where are you?"

"I'm at the house. I must've just missed you," John said. She could hear the commotion in the background. There was intermittent talking, as though someone were speaking into another telephone. Another voice yelled out orders. Then she heard her front doorbell ring, then a dog barking.

Meanwhile, Frank switched the TV on. Helen snatched the remote from him and promptly switched it off again. They glared at each other for a moment. Helen nodded in Sally's direction. She guessed that Helen wanted to shield her from seeing the house on the news. He shrugged his shoulders, sat down and picked up a fishing magazine. Helen returned to the couch and frowned at Sally, concerned.

"God, what a mess," John said. "It's chaos here."

He hasn't even asked if I'm OK. "Well, are you coming to get me?" she snapped, turning away from Helen.

"Give me a break Sally, I've just got here."

"Mr. Pringle," She heard him being called in the background.

"I can't come yet. The police want to ask me some questions," he said.

"But how much longer are you going to be?"

"Mr. Pringle, please?" said the voice.

"I have no idea. Look, I'll be there as soon as I can."

After John hung up, Sally held onto the receiver. Despite being among friends, she felt completely and utterly alone. She wished she could rewind the evening. To do something other than she had done. Gone out, been anywhere than at home.

She placed the receiver on its base. "John's at the house. He has a few things to sort out before he can pick me up." She went over to Helen and sat down beside her.

"Why don't you both spend the night here?" Helen kicked Frank on the shin and raised her eyebrows at him, demanding a response. He peered over the top of his magazine. "I was just saying that Sally and John should stay here tonight."

"Yes, of course they should," he said.

"Thanks," she said, smiling appreciatively. "That sounds like a good idea. But I'll see what John thinks when he gets here."

The phone rang again. This time Helen went to answer it.

"Did the police give you any idea about what's going on?" Frank asked, closing his magazine.

"No. They really didn't say anything. It's chaotic over there. The police are everywhere. They've even got tracker dogs."

"Well yes Joan, I have," Helen rolled her eyes. "Actually Sally's here … no she's lying down, resting. I'm sorry but I've got to go. I have to leave the line free. John might be trying to get through. OK, of course I will."

Helen replaced the receiver and came over. "She sends her love."

"You know that sounds like a good idea," Sally said.

Helen looked bewildered.

"Would you mind if I go and lie down?"

"No! No, of course not. You must be exhausted. You can use Bruce's old bedroom."

Sally got up from the couch, grabbed her bag, jacket and shoes, then followed Helen down the hallway.

"What a night?" Sally sighed.

Helen opened the door to one of her bedrooms and flicked on the light switch. "It won't seem so bad after you've had a good rest." Helen hugged her. "It'll be fine. You'll see."

Sally glanced around the room. It was characterless, more like a hotel bedroom, containing the bare minimum. Just a bed, closet and a dressing table. Even the beige, striped wallpaper seemed devoid of personality.

"Give us a shout if you need anything," Helen said.

Sally dropped her belongings on the floor as Helen closed the door. She sat on the edge of the bed and caught her reflection in the dressing table mirror. Her face was bloated and her eyes bloodshot. Not bothering to undress, she pulled back the comforter and slid beneath it. As she lay, she heard the faint sounds of a TV. Frank and Helen were probably watching the news. She closed her eyes.

6

"Sally, Sally!" shouted a voice. She was being shaken. She opened her eyes.

"John!" She sat up and hugged him.

"It's OK." He patted her back then pried her from him. "Let's go," he said, whipping the comforter away from her.

"Well, Frank and Helen have offered to …"

A gentle tap on the opened door interrupted her. It was Helen. "How are you feeling Sally?"

"Sally's fine, thank you, Helen," John answered. "I think we'll make our way home now."

"Home John? Tonight? But you're very welcome to stay the night here."

"Thank you, Helen," he said tersely. "But I don't think that'll be necessary."

Surprised by his abruptness, Sally glanced between the two. He gave Sally one of his non-negotiable expressions. She assumed that she needed to discuss something with her privately.

"Thanks for the offer Helen. But I think John's probably right." she said, swinging her legs over the side of the bed and shuffling her feet into her shoes.

John stepped back to let her go ahead of him and picked up her belongings. Helen looked concerned as they passed her in the hallway.

In the living room, Frank stood up and went over to them as they headed for the door. "You're going?"

"Yes," John said. "Thanks for looking after Sally."

"Of course, anytime," he said.

Sally trailed John to his BMW, suddenly feeling apprehensive about returning home. She held onto the car's door handle, glancing longingly at the Pearce's, who were now standing at their threshold. John was already in the car.

"Call us if you need us!" Helen shouted after them.

John retracted the window on her side. "Come on!" he beckoned. Springing into action, she quickly jumped into the front passenger seat and closed the door. He promptly reversed off the drive.

"Why didn't you want to stay?" she asked.

"I just thought we'd had enough excitement for one night, without going over it all again with the Pearce's. Besides, I think we'd get a better night's sleep in our own bed."

"Yes, I suppose you're right," she said, unconvincingly.

He shifted into drive and accelerated down the street.

"John, why would anyone want to shoot … shoot at the house?"

"Who the hell knows? Kids getting their kicks, I suppose. Darnell said as much. It's obviously a random act. We've probably got the safest house in the neighborhood now.

Can't imagine anyone, even kids, being stupid enough to hit the same house twice."

"Is that what he told you? I got the impression it was more serious than that."

"Oh, Darnell's bound to make more out of it than it really is. Probably sees a promotion in it. You know, we didn't really research this place before we moved out here," he continued. "We should've at least checked out the crime statistics."

She shifted in her seat. *I can't believe he's using the shooting to complain about living here!* "It's hardly Detroit, is it?" she snapped.

He turned into their street. "No, of course not. I'm not saying it is. But even the suburbs have their problems."

"Like what?"

"Well, Fenton's become a very expensive place to live. I'm sure a lot of families are finding it difficult to make ends meet."

"So? What's that got to do with it?" she asked.

"If both parents are at work, who knows what kids get up to while they're left on their own?"

Sally sighed.

"There's certainly not a lot for a teenager to do around here," he continued.

She mouthed the words she knew would come next.

"There isn't even a cinema!"

She didn't respond, she was too exhausted.

John pulled onto their drive. The police were now nowhere to be seen. The only trace of them being there was the broken pieces of yellow caution tape strewn across the front lawn. As they left the car, she spotted Mrs. Hernandez, her neighbor across the street, peering from behind her drapes. They stepped into the house and John switched on the hallway light. For a moment, they assessed the carnage. A couple of chairs were knocked over. Dirty footprints covered the living room floor and several used cups were on the coffee table.

She shuddered. Her short nap had left her feeling slightly detached. But now, seeing the evidence left by the police, the severity of the situation returned in spades. "Oh God," she said, closing the door.

John dropped her bag onto the floor. "Yes. It's a mess. Call the cleaners tomorrow. You're going to need some help." He headed over to the drinks cabinet.

She rubbed the coldness from her arms. "What kind of questions did the police ask?" She walked over to the toppled chairs.

"Oh, the usual police crap," He poured himself a whisky with one hand and loosened his shirt and tie with his other.

Sally righted one of the chairs. "Like what?"

"Did you attempt to kill your wife?" he said, in a droll voice.

"John! Was that supposed to be funny?"

"Sorry," he said indifferently. He swallowed his drink in one, flipping back his head as he did so.

How could he be so flippant, so callous? She straightened the other chair.

He refilled his glass. "Well, what kind of questions do you think they asked? They wanted to know where I was at the time of the shooting. You know, the usual police bullshit. Nothing to worry about."

Nothing to worry about! Doesn't he realize I could have been killed?

"John ..." she started to protest. He raised an eyebrow waiting for her to continue. She suddenly felt drained and unable to handle a confrontation. "I'm off to bed," she said turning and heading down the hallway.

"I'll be right with you!" he shouted after her. "Just need to make a few phone calls. Let Harrison know what's going on. Ask him to reschedule some of my appointments when he gets to the office in the morning. The police want to talk to us again tomorrow!"

Screw Paul Harrison! Screw work! And Screw the police! She glanced sideways at the new bedroom. The light was on. Her heart missed a beat as she replayed her frantic scramble across the floor earlier. She went into her old bedroom, switched on the light, slammed the door behind her and leant against it. She heard John's muffled voice talking on the phone. He laughed. *What on earth could he find so funny at a time like this.* She fell face down onto her bed. She felt comforted by the familiar texture and smell of the duvet cover. It smelt exactly as it did that morning, she wasn't so sure about everything else. *John's treating the shooting like it's a mere irritation. Maybe he knows more? Perhaps Darnell had told him that he thought it was kids.*

Hearing John saying goodbye and replacing the receiver, Sally sat up and started undressing. After putting on her nightclothes she slipped under the duvet. Again, she heard his voice. She suspected he was picking up messages and leaving others at work. *That's John alright, even in a crisis, he always keeps his cool.*

She turned onto her side, and remembered the day that had triggered their relationship. They had crossed paths many times, but as they worked in different departments they had only exchanged the most basic of civilities. It wasn't until he started working for Mark Bryson, Sally's boss, that fate had drawn them together.

She'd been perusing an investment portfolio for one of their most prestigious clients. Spotting a computation error, she'd called him.

"Mr. Pringle, Sally Campbell."

"Yes, Sally, what can I do for you?"

"I'm in the process of typing out the Williamson investment portfolio, and I've found an error in the yield curve forecast. I think you should take another look at it, before it's submitted to Mr. Bryson."

There'd been an intense pause before he answered. "Oh, and what seems to be the problem?"

"Your stats on page twelve. There's a mistake in your, in the calculations ..."

"So, you're familiar with CAPM theory, Miss Campbell?" he'd asked curtly.

"Well not officially. But I have typed enough of these statements for Mr. Bryson to have full confidence in me checking them over."

Again, there had been a long pause. "Mr. Pringle?"

"Yes, I'm looking at the figures now ..."

"The total in column three I believe should read 1,406,000, not 1,244,000," she said, hearing him tap away on his computer.

Not liking to be caught making a mistake he'd been curt. "Quite right, Miss Campbell. I would very much appreciate you changing it." The next time they met, he had thanked her properly and the ice had been broken.

She'd always admired his unflappable self-assurance. He never got caught up in trivialities like she tended to do and often an issue was gone before she became aware of it. She'd regarded his cool, no-nonsense attitude as a positive trait - until now.

She turned into her pillow and shut her eyes, wondering where she would be if she hadn't spotted that error ...

7

A familiar and unwelcomed sound buzzed into Sally's consciousness. Her eyelids flickered in response to the alarm clocks' irritating wail. John thwacked the clock into silence, firing up her memory of the night before. Overwhelmed, she pulled the duvet over her head.

John sat up, yawned and performed his morning head scratching ritual. "Honey it's 6:30 am," he said, patting her cocoon. "Time to make a move." The bed bounced as he stepped from it.

She stretched her limbs then unenthusiastically staggered out of bed. Her body ached from the adrenalin released from the day before. She slipped on her white toweling robe. John picked up his discarded work clothes from the floor and unceremoniously threw them onto a chair. His eyes were bloodshot – *probably from too much whiskey.*

"I could do with a strong cup of coffee," he said, disappearing into the bathroom.

"Hmmm," she mumbled disapprovingly. Leaving the bedroom, she crossed the living room, and on autopilot, headed to the front door to retrieve the morning paper from the drive. The door was unlocked. *Oh for heaven's sake! He hadn't even bothered to lock it last night!* A blast of damp, cold air hit her face and lower legs. Dan, her neighbor was walking his dog. He stopped and waved a hand in greeting, but before he could speak, she slammed the door shut. She couldn't face anyone, not yet.

She headed to the kitchen to prepare breakfast. In an attempt to distract her from thinking about the shooting, she switched on the radio. "Question four. A word beginning with B used to describe a feeling when someone is unfaithful?"

After slipping bread into the toaster, she made coffee and set the table. The room felt cold and sullied. The smell of unfamiliar people lingered. The only other time she'd felt this way was six years ago, when her car had been stolen. The police found it a week later in an abandoned warehouse, after it had been used in a bank robbery. When she went to reclaim it, the car seemed smaller than she remembered. And when she sat inside, it made her feel violated. She sold it a week later.

"If you know the answer, call three, five, five, six, treble seven. 'So come on, come on, do the locomotion with me,' " bellowed the radio.

Betrayal, thought Sally, answering the radio presenter's question. She poured herself a coffee.

"Have you seen my notebook?" John asked, striding across the living room floor. He was dressed in his suit.

"John, surely you're not going into work?" The toaster flipped up the bread. He went to the back of the sofa, scanning the floor. "Where the hell is it? Did I bring it in from the car last night?"

"John! I can't stay on my own. Not today! Not after last night!" Of course, her mom was coming, but he didn't know. Besides, she wanted him there. Surely, he realized that?

"Don't be so dramatic, Sally," He recovered his laptop from the side of the drinks cabinet.

"Dramatic!" she yelled, smashing her mug onto the counter. The hot coffee splattered her hand, making her wince. "I was shot at last night! Damn you!" She covered her face with her hands.

"Sally!"

"Don't you realize I could have been killed! Don't you care?"

"Sally," he repeated, this time softly. He went to her, put an arm around her and drew her close. "I'm sorry. What a shit! Of course, it must have been awful. I guess I've been so angry about it all, I hadn't stopped to think how you must be feeling." He kissed the top of her head.

"I was so scared. Why … why would someone do this to us?"

"Nobody's doing anything to us. It's just kids. They probably don't even know how much trouble they've caused. And it was just our bad luck they picked our house. You can't honestly think that someone intentionally tried to shoot you?" he said, stroking her hair. He eased her away and studied her face.

"Well, no," she said. "That's ridiculous. I mean why would anyone do that?"

"Exactly! I really think you're reading more into this than you should."

"But, I can't be on my own. Not today," she pleaded.

"Yes, you're right. Of course I'll stay."

He grabbed a tissue from the box on the kitchen counter and handed it to her. She dabbed her eyes and blew her nose. She felt so relieved that he had agreed to stay, she decided not to upset the applecart by telling him about her mother's impending visit yet.

"Let's get on with breakfast, shall we?" He opened the refrigerator and pulled out a carton of orange juice. "What are we having?"

"I'm having egg on toast. What would you like?"

"Sounds great," he said, picking out a glass from the kitchen cabinet.

"What? But you don't like eggs!"

John froze. Slowly, he poured juice into his glass. "I've never said that I didn't like them. I've usually just preferred something else, that's all. I think egg on toast would be nice for a change." With his juice, he went to sit at the breakfast table.

In all the years she had known him, John had never eaten eggs. Particularly since he had bad cholesterol. She took another egg from the refrigerator and stared at the back of his head, trying unsuccessfully, to recall the occasion when he had told her that he hated eggs. She cracked open the egg, poured it into the pan and threw the empty shell into the sink. "As you're not going into work today, how about taking a trip to the garden center. Choose some shrubs for the backyard?"

"Well maybe, but let's see how it goes. Sally, where's the paper?" He scanned the table, as if disbelieving it wasn't there.

"Oh yes, the paper. What an airhead. I completely forgot about it this morning." The eggs spat at her, as if scolding her for the lie. She turned down the heat.

John left the table and strode out of the front door. Fresh, cold air slithered around the bottom of her legs. She watched him walk towards the paper, wondering how he wanted his egg. As he picked up the folded newspaper from the drive, a large white van screeched to a halt against the curb. A man carrying a large camera jumped from it, followed by a woman dressed in a blue skirt suit, clutching a microphone. Sally realized it was Marjorie Myers from Channel 11 News. Then another news van pulled up across the street.

John quickly picked up the paper and rushed back inside with Marjorie hot on his tail. "Mr. Pringle! Mr. Pringle, Channel 11 News. I wonder if you could spare a few moments!"

He slammed the door in her face.

"The press are here!" he said. The doorbell rang.

They stood transfixed, glaring at the door as though a monster were on the other side.

"What shall we do?" Sally asked

Someone was firmly pressing the doorbell. Its incessant ring and John's failure to answer scared her. The situation seemed bigger than both of them.

He strode to the kitchen and turned up the volume on the radio.

"Ignore them!" he shouted.

Sally flattened her hands against her ears, as Whitney Houston burst from the radio. "And ... I ... will always love you ... oo ... oooo."

John then marched over to the doorbell and opened the plastic cover. He pulled at the wires until they broke free from the connector, instantly killing the sound of the bell. He returned to the table and unfolded the newspaper. "Look here!" he yelled.

He held up the paper. She read '*More shootings in Fenton!*' She turned down the volume on the radio, then scooped his fried egg onto a slice of toast.

"The press have really gone to town over these so-called shootings," he scoffed. "It's just small town mentality. Someone probably trying to sabotage the new housing development by stirring up bad press."

"You know that's exactly what Helen said yesterday." She placed his breakfast in front of him. John put down the paper and poked his egg with his knife. He then dipped a piece of toast in the yoke. It was the first time she had ever seen him eat an egg. Just as he was about to take a bite, he suddenly paused and glanced up at her.

"Is there any coffee?" he asked, dismissively.

"Yes ... Yes, of course." She went back to the kitchen.

Pounding started on the front door.

"Took them awhile to work out the bell's broken," John sniggered. "Not exactly high IQ."

"Do you think they'll go away?"

"Eventually, I guess."

Sally filled his cup. She placed the coffeepot on the table and held onto the back of his chair. "But don't you think we should talk to them? I mean, it's not as though we've done anything?" John didn't answer. He continued eating. "And it might make them go away," she said.

A flash of light from outside caught her attention. A man with a camera stood in their back garden by the broken fence. "Oh my God, someone's taking pictures of us!" She grasped the top of her bathrobe, and looked down at the floor embarrassed.

"Really, this is too much!" John shot out of his chair. "Get dressed! We'll have to put a stop to this."

Nervously, she glanced toward the garden again. The man had gone. *Oh God. I'm going to be in the paper in my robe!* She followed John to the bedroom. He sat down at his desk.

"What are you doing?' Sally opened her drawer, pulled out underwear and started dressing.

"Writing a statement."

She slipped on a pair of yellow Capri's and pulled a blue and white striped T-shirt from her closet. The phone rang. John sprang from his desk and answered it from the bedside table. "Hello?" He listened a moment then slammed down the receiver so hard it made her flinch.

"Who was that?" she asked, zipping up her Capri's.

"Another reporter. This is crazy!"

Sally had never seen him like this. He seemed vulnerable and she found it unsettling. Again, the phone rang. He glared at it but didn't move.

"I'll get it." Quickly, she slipped the T-shirt over her head, and picked up the phone. "Hello?" she said, nervously.

"Sally, it's Helen."

"Oh Helen." Relieved, she sat on the bed.

John returned to his desk.

"Are you OK?" Helen asked. "You sound strange?"

"Yes, I'm fine. I'm just glad it's you. We've just had a call from a reporter. I thought they were calling again."

"Is there anything I can do to help? Would you like me to come over?"

"Thank you Helen, but no, we're fine." She picked up her sandals by the side of the bed and slipped them on with her free hand. John turned and held up the statement.

"I'm sorry Helen, I've got to go. Can I call you later?"

"Sure."

After replacing the receiver, she picked up her brush from the side of the phone and ran it through her hair.

John got up from his desk. "Are you ready?"

"Ready? Ready for what?" She put down the brush.

"To talk to the press!" he shrugged his shoulders and held out his arms in disbelief.

"Oh, no John, I couldn't," she said, shaking her head.

"But it was your idea!"

"I know. I just thought that … that you would do it. I can't face them."

"But you're the one in the spotlight. You were the one who was shot at. They'll want to hear from you!"

Sally jumped up from the bed. *Oh, how could he! Minutes ago he'd said it was just a random shooting. Now he was saying that I was shot at!* The pounding on the door seemed louder, menacing. "It was the house that was shot at, remember! Not me! I just happened to be here at the time. If you had been here, would you say that you had been shot at?" Her body trembled with fear and anger.

"Of course not. Sally, I'm sorry. It was a bad choice of words." He stepped nearer. Impulsively, she stepped back, not wanting him to touch her.

"But honey," he said, softly. "They won't be satisfied until they see you. I'll do all the talking. You can just stand by me. I really think it's better if you come out there with me."

Brusquely, she wiped hot angry tears from her eyes. Of course, he was right. He always was. She knew that the press wouldn't leave until they had seen her. And it would be best to get it over with now than to have them outside the house every day.

She glared at his outstretched hand, not wanting to go with him, but knowing she must.

"Sally?" he pleaded.

"Alright, but make it short," she snapped.

She took his hand and with the statement, he led her through the house to the front door. But before opening it, he peered through the spy hole. "Oh!"

"What is it? Have they gone?" she asked hopefully.

"No. It's the cops. The ones from last night. And they don't look very happy. It must've been them making all that racket." He opened the door. Immediately, a chorus of camera lenses flashed behind the officers.

"Would you mind … letting us in?" Inspector Darnell asked coolly.

"Yes, of course," John said. Sally let go of his hand and retreated into the living room, allowing Darnell, Mary, and another uniformed police officer she didn't recognize, to enter. The press gushed forward, camera lenses flashed vigorously again.

"Mr. Pringle, what do you think? … How's your wife?" shouted voices from the crowd.

"OK, OK guys, back off," Darnell told the mob.

John stepped in front of him and addressed the crowd. "My wife and I are willing to give a statement," he said. This seemed to pacify them. They stopped pushing and fell silent.

Darnell retreated into the house. John turned to Sally and waved her over. She hesitated, glancing at the police officers, hoping they would advise her against it. But all she got was a sympathetic look from Mary.

"Come on, Sally!" John demanded, frantically waving her over. As she neared the door, he reached out and pulled her forward, cradling her with his arm. Immediately, an army of flashing cameras assaulted her face. Her mind, overwhelmed with stimulus, slowed her senses to a snail's pace. She saw mouths move, but there was no sound. Everything seemed disjointed and exaggerated, like a movie sticking to its reel, unable to move from one frame to another. Even the flashes from the cameras seemed sluggish, their radiance dispersing a little at a time.

Why are these people standing on our front lawn taking pictures of us? Why had someone tried to shoot me? She stared at John's hand. *Why is John's arm around my shoulder, gripping me so tightly? And why, after four years of marriage, had he suddenly started eating eggs?* She glanced up at his face, then back at the crowd. Another camera lens flashed, this time directly in her eyes. Cognizant but dazed, she faced the ground. John tightened his grip. "Sally, Sally," he whispered, prompting her to face the crowd again.

"We really don't have much to tell you," John finally addressed them. "We're assuming, until the police say otherwise, that last night's incident was the consequence of a student prank. We also understand, that similar happenings have occurred over the past two weeks. Of course, we are upset by the incident and the police have promised to get to the bottom of this as soon as they can. That's all we have to say right now."

"How are you feeling, Mrs. Pringle?" A reporter yelled.

John squeezed her shoulder.

"Oh, I'm fine," she answered, nervously. "A little shaken, but fine." She smiled faintly, instigating a renewed onslaught of camera flashes.

"Now as you can probably appreciate, this has been a distressing experience for both of us," John said. "We ask that you please respect our privacy and now leave us in peace."

Several microphones assaulted their faces, followed by a barrage of questions. "Did you hear? ... What have the police?" ... Sally and John stepped back into the hallway. "Mrs. Pringle, Mrs. Pringle! ..." John pushed the door shut.

They both sighed heavily. "Now, how can we help you?" John said, turning to Darnell.

"First, we would like to take ..." started Darnell. Then there was another knock on the door.

"Won't they ever give up? Can't you do something about this?" John snapped at Darnell, who merely shrugged his shoulders. He yanked open the door, while Sally peered over his shoulder. There stood Mike, Andy, and Matt.

"What the hell is going on?' Mike asked. Cameras were held high in the air, frantically flashing, trying to get additional shots of John and Sally over the workmen's heads.

"Back off, will ya?" Andy yelled to someone pushing against him. Mike swung around and pushed the reporter standing behind him, who promptly lost his balance. The crowd of reporters tumbled like dominoes, some impaling themselves on the now completely bare rose bushes, but most fell on top of each other on the front lawn. There were shouts and screams. Pleased with himself, Mike strutted serenely past John, followed closely by a very amused Andy and Matt. Mike suddenly stopped in front of the two uniformed cops, where his smug, regal grin, promptly died.

Darnell gave Mike a contemptuous scowl and went over to see what had happened. But instead of getting angry, his face lit up when he saw the scene. "Pete! Mary!" he shouted. "Check this out!" The two officers joined him at the door and they all started chuckling. Sally peered over Darnell's shoulder. An annoyed reporter demanded that Mike be arrested for grievous bodily harm. "Damaged goods," shouted a photographer who looked suspiciously like the one who had taken photos of John and herself from the backyard.

"Marjorie! I didn't know you were a 'Victoria Secrets' girl. The guys at the station will be impressed," Pete sniggered. Marjorie, Channel 11's anchorwoman, was lucky to be on top of the pile of reporters but simultaneously unlucky that her skirt had risen to her waist, showing off a red pair of panties. She looked pretty comical as she writhed around on top of the reporters, trying unsuccessfully to secure her footing.

"You could really hurt yourself, tripping over like that," Mary said. Sally had the feeling that the officers were imparting some overdue retribution.

Marjorie finally found her footing. She was clearly upset. Her heavily lacquered hair stuck up, like she'd had an electric shock. She pulled down her skirt and marched away, toward the street, tripping slightly over her own feet and initiating another chorus of laughter from the officers.

"Now, watch how you go," Darnell said, sarcastically. The officers were still grinning when they re-entered the house. John closed the door.

The builders still hadn't been told what was going on. "You haven't heard?" Sally started to explain. "Someone shot at our house last night."

"Sally, I don't think the workmen should concern themselves with this! I'm sure they have plenty to do," John said dismissively.

The builders merely shrugged their shoulders and sauntered off down the hallway to the back of the house.

Then John turned to Sally. "How about some coffee!" There was an officious tone to his voice. Although she knew he wasn't purposely trying to belittle her, she felt small as the officers watched her reaction to his overly brusque manner.

"Oh, yes." Sally headed to the kitchen, wondering why John was suddenly so tense.

"Shall we sit down?" John asked.

Darnell nodded to Pete and Mary, who instantly took off through the patio door. John looked to Darnell for an explanation.

"My officers need to take a look outside," he said. "They need to go over the crime scene again, now that it's daylight. If … that's OK with you?"

"Yes, of course." John motioned him over to the living room.

Sally threw the used coffee filter into the sink and inserted a fresh one into the coffee maker. The two men sat, John on the couch and Darnell opposite in the armchair. She poured fresh coffee beans into the grinder and held down the button, momentarily overpowering the silence with a short, sharp buzz.

"I won't keep you long, Mr. Pringle," Darnell said. "I just need to clarify a few details." He pulled out a notepad and pen from the inside of his suit jacket and read over some notes. Sally poured the ground coffee powder into the coffee machine, water into its well, and switched it on.

"Last night, you told me you called your wife at approximately 9:00 pm is that correct?" Darnell asked.

"Yes. As I told you, I called home to let Sally know that I'd be staying overnight at our apartment."

"Do you often stay away from home during the week?"

"When my workload demands it, yes"

"And how often is that, Mr. Pringle?"

"Quite a lot recently."

Sally opened the cupboard above her. *Why is Darnell so interested in John's work schedule?* She stood on her tiptoes, straining to reach the nicer mugs at the back of the cupboard.

"Perhaps I should rephrase the question," Darnell said sternly. "How often do you actually come home during the week?"

She accidentally nudged a small cup in the front of the cupboard. It fell, bounced once on the floor and smashed. The two men glanced over. She felt herself redden. "Sorry!"

"Well, Mr. Pringle?"

She got a brush and pan from underneath the sink, and swept up the debris.

John straightened his posture. "Well, it varies considerably. But I would say, in the last two months, not very much. I'm managing a prestigious account at the moment which demands my full attention."

Not risking any more cups, Sally picked out three clean mugs from the dishwasher and set them on a tray. Besides them, she placed the filter jug containing the freshly brewed coffee, and a milk jug from the refrigerator. Noticing that the two men had gone quiet, she glanced over to them. Darnell was visibly annoyed by John's evasiveness.

John must have realized it too. "Perhaps ten to twelve times in the last month," he said, coughing nervously into his fist. "Apart from weekends, of course."

She took the loaded tray over to them, setting it down on the coffee table. "How do you take your coffee, detective?"

"Black, thank you."

She poured the coffee and placed the mugs in front of the two men. Then she poured another for herself and sat down beside John.

"When you telephoned your wife, did you call from your office or from your apartment?" Darnell asked. He kept his head down and scribbled notes as John spoke.

"From the apartment." John moved toward the detective's notepad, straining to see what he was writing.

"From a cell phone, or from a landline?" Darnell suddenly glanced up at him.

John sat back. She suspected that he was feeling uncomfortable. He wasn't used to others dominating conversations. "I believe I called from my cell phone. Yes, that's right. I actually called Sally as I entered the elevator."

Darnell nodded and took a quick sip of his coffee. "Can anyone verify your whereabouts from say, 8:00 pm to 10 pm?"

"Look, you asked me this last night. Are you insinuating that I had something to do with this?"

"Mr. Pringle, these are just routine questions."

John sprang out of his chair. "Shouldn't you be visiting local high schools or something, questioning kids? Not harassing us like this. You know, we're the victims here!"

"Please sit down, Mr. Pringle," he said coolly.

John did as he was told. She glanced between the two men. *This is a nightmare.* She covered her face with her hands. "It's like a bad dream," she said. "One minute everything's normal and the next someone shoots at our window and everything's turned upside-down."

"Can't you see you're upsetting my wife?" John said, sitting down and placing an arm around her shoulder.

"Mr. Pringle, Mrs. Pringle. These are simply routine questions. Ninety-nine percent of the time this type of crime is solved by simple elimination. Now, I know how it looks, but please believe me, this is standard procedure. And the quicker you co-operate, the quicker we can find the person who did this."

"Then let me reiterate detective, I was with my boss until about 8:30 pm, but after that no. I picked up a burger from Hagan's, on Market, caught a cab and headed straight to my apartment."

"Your bosses name, Mr. Pringle. Where can I reach him?"

"Paul Harrison. His direct line is four one five, six eight nine, six four, two four."

"I'm sorry, Mrs. Pringle, but I have to ask you a few more questions," Darnell said gently.

She nodded OK.

"Are there any other details you can think of that need to be added to your statement? Any background information, for instance?"

Given the line of questioning today and from the night before, she assumed that he was referring to John and their lifestyle. "No. Not that I can think of," she said, shaking her head.

"Have you noticed any suspicious characters on the street, strange vehicles, or a group of kids that you've never seen before?

"No, there are only very young children and retired people living on the street. I'm sure I'd notice if a group of teenagers started hanging out here."

"OK." Darnell scratched his nose with a forefinger. "Well, that's all for now." He put his notepad and pen away in his jacket and got to his feet.

Both John and Sally stood up with him.

"Wait a second," John exclaimed. "You've asked us a lot of questions, how about bringing us up to date?"

"Well, there's not much to report right now," Darnell explained. "This was one of three incidents that occurred last night. One shot was fired from a BB gun. We believe the shots in this incident and the one on Swanson Avenue were fired from a .22 rifle. It's used by teens to hunt rodents and shoot Coke cans with. As you probably know, there's been a number of random shootings during the past two weeks. It's puzzling though and doesn't follow any psychological profile that I've ever come across."

"So, it could be high school kids firing indiscriminately," John asked.

Darnell shrugged his shoulders. "Your guess is as good as mine. But all the same, it's serious, and we're lucky so far that no-one's been seriously hurt."

He then turned to Sally. "If you remember anything else, anything at all, call me." He glanced furtively at John, then handed her his card. "And I'll be sure to keep you both informed if we learn anything else." With that he disappeared into the backyard.

"See," John said. "Darnell won't say outright, but reading between the lines, he thinks that it's kids. I told you there was nothing to worry about. I'm going to call work."

"OK," she said, smiling weakly.

He picked up the telephone and started dialing. She watched the detective through the patio door. He was talking to Pete. *Was that what Darnell had insinuated?* She tried to recall his exact words. He'd said the case was puzzling.

But as far as she could work out, he'd neither confirmed nor negated the high school prank theory.

"Hi, Leslie, it's John."

John had always been able to read people so well. But she failed to see how he could've picked up that Darnell had come to any decision regarding the case.

Outside, Darnell and Pete bent down and inspected the ground. Mike, Matt, and Andy sat on overturned wooden crates. Andy poured Mike a drink from his thermos. They were watching the police officers, obviously intrigued. Mike must have made a derogatory comment about Mary, because she straightened and glowered at him. Mike chuckled. Darnell approached the workmen. Sally heard him say something about "evidence" and "crime scene," so they promptly drank up and disappeared inside.

"Found anything, Pete?" Darnell asked, walking over to him.

Mary scoffed under her breath. She knew he wouldn't ask her. Pete and Darnell were drinking buddies. This was a closed shop, as far as she was concerned.

"No, nothing. I think forensics picked up everything last night. He glanced over the garden. "It's clean, a couple of old footprints here and there, nothing else."

Darnell squatted down and inspected the footprints. "Shit!" He stood up and from his trouser suit pocket took out a packet of cigarettes and a lighter. He offered Pete a cigarette but he declined.

"Chief pressuring you?"

"I'm too old for this game, Pete. The politics gets you in the end." He placed a cigarette between his lips and lit it, producing a plume of blue smoke.

Mary scoured the ground behind where the fence had stood. She was feeling pretty sorry for herself. Yet again she'd been passed over for promotion. *Maybe, I just haven't got what it takes.*

"What do you think of this guy?" Darnell asked Pete. nodding in the direction of the house.

"You mean, apart from being a complete a-hole?"

He smiled. "Yeah, that's what I thought. But I think he's hiding something though. It's hard to tell with these professional types."

Still, Pete wasn't exactly the brightest spark at the station, thought Mary. *How had he managed to get through this time?*

"You notice how clean all these crime scenes are?" Darnell said. "I mean, high school kids would leave evidence all over the place. Yet, every one's squeaky clean, almost professional. But then, why use a .22 and why shoot up the neighborhood with a BB gun?"

"Fucked if I know," Pete said.

Mary wandered amongst some concrete debris. Someone had smashed up an old path and dumped it at the back of the fence. Something blue caught her eye. At first, she assumed it was a broken piece of ceramic. She squatted and picked it up. Immediately realizing that she may have compromised evidence, she closed her hand around it.

92

"You got something there, Mary?" Darnell shouted.

Mary felt herself redden. She opened up her hand, immediately recognizing what it was.

"No, nothing. I just dropped my inhaler." She held it in front of her mouth and moved her finger up and down, pretending to give her mouth a quick squirt. "There's some fresh footprints back here, though," she said nervously.

Darnell sauntered over and looked down at the prints.

"Pete! Take a shot of this and make a cast for the lab," he ordered. So relieved that he had bought her lie, she didn't care that he had given the job to Pete.

Darnell walked away. "Then head back to the station."

Pete walked over to her with a smug grin on his face. What's that brown stain on your nose, she wanted to say. But she didn't, she never did.

8

Tired, pissed off and intensely bored, Tony slouched in his chair with his legs crossed at his ankles. As usual, the lecture was excruciatingly tedious and longwinded, but any distraction was a welcomed break from thinking about his fuck up the night before.

This time, aborting the hit was not only irritating and embarrassing but the police will now be on it like 'flies on horseshit' if they suspect that the shooting was anything other than random vandalism by juvenile delinquents.

"Until recently, it was considered sufficient to seek medical advice, undergo tests and receive the right kind of medication to control one's allergy or asthma attack," said Dr. Keller. The white-coated doctor sat surrounded by a dozen or so of his patients. "However, because of rising health care costs, intensive research has been undertaken in order to reveal why an individual suddenly becomes sensitive to certain allergens."

Thinking how meaningless Dr. Keller's life was, Tony nodded off.

The sound of a door slamming brought him abruptly back to life. He sat up and glanced over his shoulder. It was Mary, the woman who'd kept him awake at night and the only reason he continued to attend these dull group therapy sessions. She wore a short, black skirt and a white, thin cotton blouse. Her heels tapped starkly on the tiled surface, as her fine, smooth legs glided across the floor. She pulled out one of the chairs, its metal legs screeched loudly against the floor, attracting everyone's attention. Blushing, she glanced at Dr. Keller and mouthed an apology. As she sat, her skirt slid higher up her thighs. Everyone, except Tony, returned his or her attention to the doctor. Tony, situated at a twenty degree angle to Mary, shuffled his chair to his right in order to get a better view of her, attracting Martha, his neighbor's attention. She followed his line of sight, then fired him a contemptuous scowl.

Mary placed her purse on the floor and pulled down her skirt with a cute little bounce in her chair.

"Dr. Gerardo Fuentes of the University of Kentucky, wrote a paper in 1989 on his findings," the doctor continued. "He suggested that, as well as the usual culprits; pollution, animal dander, seasonal allergies, cosmetics etc, causes generally brought on by our environment, allergic reactions can also be brought on by stress. He specifically indicated that both long-term stress conditions, such as continuing problems at work and acute short-term stress, as in a shock, for example, the death of a loved one …"

"Yes, Hilary?" Dr. Keller suddenly said. All heads turned to her. She had her hand raised.

95

"My cat died," Hilary said softly, babyishly. She held her head to one side like a kindergarten child. It may have been cute 60 years ago, but now she looked like some deranged mental case. A few members of the group giggled.

Hilary had coarse, bleached blonde hair. Her face had been lifted so much that her skin appeared laminated over her cheekbones. At the first meeting, when they had been prompted to say a few words about themselves, she told them that she had been married and divorced five times and had come to the conclusion that animals made much better companions than men. To date, she has two parrots, one dog, a hamster and now it seemed, a dead Persian cat.

"What's your cat got to do with it?" sniggered Sam, a retired barman from Chicago. He wore a black T-shirt with Harley Davidson written across the front. He had either bought it when he was much thinner or it had shrunk in the wash, since it failed to cover his flabby, anemic looking, hairy stomach – *trash*.

Offended, Hillary straightened and batted her heavily mascaraed lashes at him. "Archibald was like my child. He was eighteen years old when he died."

Total fruitcake, thought Tony.

"Archibald! Archibald," Sam taunted, laughing and glancing at the others' reaction.

There were chuckles all around.

"Oh, how rude," she replied, squirting her inhaler into her mouth.

"Everyone has their own emotional pain limits," Dr. Keller interjected. "Attachments to animals can be as strong as attachments to humans."

Sam rolled his eyes and chuckled.

Morons the lot of them, thought Tony. *Why did he do this to himself?* He returned his attention to Mary. *That's why.* She caught his eye, blushed and then turned to face the doctor again. Feeling pleased with himself, he also returned his attention to the doctor.

"So Dr. Fuentes suggests that loss of a family member....... or an animal," said the doctor, "can put stress on the body and could conceivably precipitate an allergic reaction. Today, I would like each of you to consider whether stress could be a contributing factor of your own allergy or asthma condition. I have a questionnaire, based on Dr. Fuentes' findings ..."

Tony took a questionnaire from the pile handed to him and passed the rest along, reflecting on the futility of starting a relationship. After all, he hadn't exactly been lucky in the love department. Oh, he had no problem with sex. In that respect, he regarded himself as pretty damned good. But emotional intimacy was an entirely different matter. He believed the only way he could function professionally was to rid himself of all human emotion. Unfortunately, this wasn't something he was able to switch on and off at will.

Up until now, his short-term, noncommittal sexual interludes had been convenient and satisfying. They were uncomplicated, required no emotional or financial commitment, and didn't last long enough to risk discovery of his true profession.

However, with the death of his mother, his life had been turned upside-down. He was no longer interested in sex, and quite suddenly, his job failed to give him the satisfaction he had enjoyed for the past 15 years. He began thinking about life's biggest questions. What was it all about? For what possible reason did humans exist? It was also around this time that he started experiencing asthma attacks.

From the very beginning, Tony thought these group therapy sessions were a load of bollocks. But he'd been intrigued by his strong attraction to Mary. It had been a long time since he'd been aroused by anything, and he felt compelled to investigate further. Besides, he couldn't go anywhere. He had this last job to do.

"So, between now and next week," Keller continued, checking his watch, "please complete the questionnaire, and I will use Dr. Fuentes' methods to determine whether there are any stress related factors causing your allergic condition. The plan will then be to set up individualized therapy sessions to investigate the problem further. And now, to my favorite part of therapy, coffee!"

People slowly left their seats and drifted to the snack table. As Tony was nearest, he got there first and poured himself a coffee.

"Hi," said a female voice from behind. Turning, he couldn't believe his luck. It was Mary.

"Hi," he replied. For the first time in his life he felt himself blush – *What the hell?*

She stepped beside him and picked up an empty cup and saucer. "So, what do you think about the doctor's theory?"

"There may be something to it." He picked up the coffeepot and motioned to fill her cup.

"Oh, thank you," she said.

She smelled musky. He had a hard time not looking down her blouse. His hand shook slightly as he filled her cup. He felt his trouser tackle stir, and felt relieved that it was not permanently damaged. He replaced the pot on the table. "What do you think about the theory?" He placed a cookie on his saucer.

"Oh, I'm open to any theory that'd rid me of my asthma. And my mother, God bless her soul," she made the sign of the cross, across her chest, "said I was a born worrier."

"Your mother's dead?" he asked, biting into the cookie.

"Yes, heart attack, last year."

"Oh." He wanted to tell her that his mother had recently died. He hadn't told anyone. He hadn't anyone to tell. But he didn't.

"Although right now my biggest problem's work. It's so stressful and I'm beginning to think I'm not cut out for it." She stared into space, as if pondering more about what she had said.

"Oh. So what is it?" he asked, sipping his coffee.

"What?"

"Your job? What do you do?" he asked again.

"Oh, I'm a cop."

He spluttered his coffee.

"Hey, steady on," she said, patting his back.

"Sorry," he croaked. "Got … I got a piece of cookie stuck."

She offered him a napkin.

"Thank you." He wiped his shirt.

Realizing that he'd also spluttered her blouse, he motioned to wipe it. "Oh ... Er," he said, his hand hovering over her chest.

"Oh, don't worry about that ..." She promptly placed her cup on the table and grabbed the napkin from him. "It'll wash."

"What do you do?" she asked, blotting the stain from her blouse. "By the way," she said, holding out her hand, "I'm Mary....Mary Bruin."

He held her long, soft, cool hand. "David Sullivan. I work in security," he said, immediately wishing he hadn't. It sounded far too boring.

"Really!" she said, removing her hand from his and picking up her cup again. "I've been thinking about moving into that myself. I'm kinda disillusioned with the police force. I keep getting passed over for promotion and I guess the security business would be a natural choice, after the police service."

"OK guys, let's move on," shouted Dr. Keller. Mary quickly swallowed her coffee and returned her empty cup to the table. Tony followed suit, accidentally brushing his arm against hers. She glanced up at his face and blushed. Although their eyes only met for a split second, the moment seemed like a lifetime. Her eyes were deep green, like grass.

"I know this is kinda forward," she said, "but can I call you? I would love to find out more about the security business."

Is she for real? I'm actually being picked up.

"Sure!"

She plucked a pen and a piece of paper from her purse, and he dictated his cell phone number. "I suppose we should go and take our seats," she said, smiling. Tony trailed after her, trying unsuccessfully to suppress a grin.

Dr. Keller asked them to rearrange their chairs, so they could watch a video. Tony tried to sit beside Mary, but Martha beat him to it, so he opted to sit behind her. This way he could stare at her as much as he liked. *What the hell am I thinking, she's a cop!*

9

John kissed Sally goodbye at the door and shot down the front garden path. He'd told her he was going into work for a couple of hours to sign some documents. Although he'd promised not to be long, she made it clear she was not happy about it. But John seemed totally convinced that high school kids were behind the shootings and there was now nothing to worry about. At least the media had left.

"I've done all there is to do here," he'd said. "I've dealt with the police, the press and anyway, this whole thing's been blown way out of proportion. There's no point in hanging around here waiting for the police to finish their investigation. It could take weeks! Besides, I'll be back before you know it."

Sally watched him reverse off the drive. She spotted Mrs. Hernandez at her window. Sally waved to John as he drove off, then closed the door.

It had been such a busy morning, but now that the police, glass-fitters, cleaners, and workmen had gone, the house seemed eerily quiet.

Realizing she'd forgotten to tell John about her mother's impending visit, she rushed to the phone. She dialed the first couple of numbers of his cell, but then had second thoughts. *If I tell him he'd be sure to stay overnight in the city.* After replacing the receiver, she noticed a number of messages on the answering machine. Sally pressed the replay button. "Hello, this is Shirley Staples from KNBC … Hello, Mrs. Pringle this is Marshall Lowe, CHB." She systematically erased them but stopped when she recognized a familiar voice. "Hi, Sally, it's Helen again. I've had calls from the girls. Of course, they've heard about last night. Anyway, we're getting together this afternoon, and I told them I'd invite you over. I thought maybe you'd want to get out of that goldfish bowl over there. But if you're not up to it, I'm sure they'll understand. Anyway, they'll be here around noon if you can make it. Take care. Bye."

Sally turned to the kitchen clock; it was already 12:20. She glanced around the empty house, and without another thought, grabbed her keys and left.

As soon as Sally turned into Helen's street and spotted Joan's car parked in Helen's driveway, she realized her mistake. She'd be in for a barrage of questions and what she needed was a distraction, not an interrogation. She should've gone shopping instead, and thinking she still could, she drove into Helen's neighbors' driveway in order to turn around. But it was too late. Helen was at her front window, looking bewildered, clearly wondering what she was doing. Feeling trapped, she reversed then parked up against the curb in front of her house.

As Sally approached Helen's front door, she told herself that her anxiety was unfounded. These were her friends, and she was sure to spend a fun afternoon with them. But, before she had time to press the doorbell, the door sprang open.

"Oh, how are you?" Joan asked, lunging forward and hugging her tightly.

"Fine. Really, I'm fine," Sally's anxiety immediately returned in spades. As soon as Joan released her, she hurried inside, her friend hot on her tail. Joan didn't stop for breath. "Well, fancy this kind of thing happening in Fenton. I mean, it really makes you think about your neighbors, doesn't it?"

Rachael, Marie, and Helen were standing to attention in the middle of the living room, as though they were greeting some dignitary, further increasing her anxiety.

"As I said to Eric, we should complain to the city about …" Joan ranted on.

"Hi," Sally greeted the others.

"… not enough police here," babbled Joan.

Marie sighed and rolled her eyes at Joan. "Give it a rest, Joan. Let the poor woman sit down."

"How are you? We've been so worried about you," Rachael said.

Both Rachael and Marie sat down on the couch like a pair of Siamese twins.

"It all seems quite unreal." Sally dropped into the high-backed chair across from them and Joan went to fetch herself a chair from the dining room. Helen meanwhile, propped herself against the fireplace.

"It's like I'm in some cheap, tacky movie. If this is my fifteen minutes of fame, I'll be glad when it's over."

"So do the police have any idea who did it?" Rachael asked.

Sally shrugged her shoulders. "Well, of course the police think it's connected to the other incidents. But they aren't saying much, and it's still early days."

"I don't know about you girls, but I don't feel safe at night anymore," Joan declared. They all nodded in agreement. "So, you don't think it's personal then?"

"Oh, really Joan!" Marie snapped.

The others seemed shocked by her remark, but turned to Sally for an answer. Nobody but Joan, had the guts to ask, but it was obvious that they all had the same question on their minds. "Of course not. That's ridiculous!" Sally snapped.

"Oh dear," Joan said. "I'm so sorry. I didn't mean anything by that, I..."

Helen moved off the fireplace. "Sally, how about helping me with some drinks?"

Sally followed Helen into the kitchen, she heard Marie scolding Joan for being tactless.

"Thanks," Sally said to Helen.

"Anytime. You know, she's all heart."

"Yes, I know, but sensitivity is not Joan's strongest point," Sally said.

"No, it certainly isn't. Can you imagine this happening to her? The dramatics, the fainting?" Helen mocked a faint. They laughed. She turned, opened a cupboard and brought out several mugs.

"Of course, nothing like this would happen to Miss Perfect," Sally said. "Over 30 years of blissful marriage to the perfect man, to produce the perfect son. We all know Joan's a pain in the backside …" She suddenly became aware of the frozen expression on Helen's face. She was frowning and staring straight past her.

Sally turned and saw Joan standing behind her.

"Oh, Joan …"

"It's OK." Joan's hand motioned Sally to be quiet. "I know what you all think. How could you not? I've been so dammed prissy over the years."

Sally glanced at Helen for support.

"But you're quite wrong … about Eric and myself. We're not perfect. All of its been a sick, twisted lie."

"Joan," Sally pleaded.

Again Joan's hand silenced her. "No, let me explain. I'm not the perfect wife. It's all been a front. And I'm so tired of it. You see a long time ago, I had an affair."

Dumbfounded, Sally glanced at Helen. Her face was expressionless but her eyes were firmly fixed on Joan.

"It was years ago, someone I met at work, when we lived in Atlanta," Joan continued.

Sally moved to Helen's side. Joan had a faraway look, as though she could see the past right before her eyes.

"Larry, the other man, was my boss. He was married with two small children and I was only 20 at the time. He used me, of course, said he was going to leave his wife and kids. You know, the usual rubbish." She laughed, but there was pain in her eyes. "Then a friend of his wife's saw us one evening and all hell let loose. I was so naive. I mean he had a family, commitments. But by that time, I was pregnant."

"With Joseph?" Helen asked. Joan nodded yes.

"Joan! Please, you don't have to tell us this." Sally said.

"I didn't know who the father was," Joan continued, "and paternity tests didn't exist in those days. And I didn't know! He could have been Eric's, but then again … Anyway, it didn't matter. As far as Eric was concerned, he'd forget it ever happened. He said Joseph was his, and that would be the end of it! He was…. and still is, a wonderful father to Joseph. They speak to each other on the phone almost every day, but with me…….well, that's a different matter," she said, smiling tearfully. "For more than 30 years he's put me through living hell. Insisting he knew where I was every minute of the day. He'd called me randomly from work, just to make sure I was where I was supposed to be."

"So that's why you never stay here long?" Helen said.

"I've even caught him following me in the car, when I went out at night. You see I had to be the perfect wife, because I owed him, didn't I?" Joan turned to Sally. "You want to know why I'm such a pain in the ass? Well, I'll tell you. I was so busy performing the perfect wife, I don't even know who I am anymore."

"Oh, Joan I'm so sorry," Sally said.

"Why didn't you leave him?" Helen asked evenly.

Sally knew what Helen was thinking. She'd done it, so why hadn't Joan?

"Guilt, duty, my upbringing, I don't know. And it wasn't so easy back in those days, particularly if you were pregnant. And you know, that saying 'It's not over till it's over?' About

107

two months ago, quite suddenly, Eric stopped checking up on me. When I asked him why he hadn't been calling, he said he had other things on his mind."

Sally was oblivious to what Joan was insinuating.

"Another woman." Helen said.

"So it's alright now, you see." Joan smiled bitterly through her tears. "I'm free of him. No more calls. Doesn't follow me anymore. It's perfect now. Just like a regular marriage, don't you think?"

Lost for words, Sally glanced at Helen, hoping she would come up with something.

"I'd better go," Joan said, suddenly leaving the kitchen.

"No Joan, don't go. Please stay," Helen shouted, trailing her.

Sally followed them both out of the kitchen. Joan was already by the door, putting on her jacket, when she reached the living room.

"Joan, stay. Please!" Helen tried again.

Rachael and Marie were giggling about something.

"Hey, you're going? So soon?" Marie shouted.

"Yes. I've got things to do," Joan said, smiling appreciatively at Helen, then left.

"Well, who would have thought," Helen said.

"What?" Marie asked. She glanced at Sally. "What?" she repeated.

"Oh, I feel so awful," Sally said.

"Don't blame yourself," Helen replied. "I think she wanted to get it off her chest."

Rachael and Marie glanced at each other, bemused.

10

Hot, sticky, and ahead of schedule, Sylvia Freeman stood on the sidewalk, outside San Francisco International Airport. The cab driver picked up her bags and loaded them into the trunk, while she slid into the backseat of the cab.

"Where to?" asked the driver, as he squeezed behind the steering wheel.

"East Bay, Fenton," she told him, pulling off her sweater. The cab driver slammed his door shut and pulled briskly away from the curb.

Sylvia opened her compact and fingered through her short cropped, gray hair. She tried combing it to the left, but the tufts stubbornly sprang back to attention. Her hair had only just started to grow back after an unsuccessful round of chemo and wasn't long enough to style. It felt soft, silky and liberated from years of hair dye. Her ex-business partners would probably not have recognized her; she hardly recognized herself. Again, she felt a twinge of rejection over her former business partners failure to return her calls. She felt particularly wounded by Gerald, her oldest and most loyal colleague and now the new chairman of Freeman

Enterprises. She assumed he felt awkward about her illness. But still, it hurt. She snapped the compact shut, as the cab accelerated onto Highway 101.

It must be at least 90°F outside, a rarity for San Francisco. She'd have to change out of her jeans, as soon as she reached Sally's. She asked the driver to turn up the air conditioning, then settled back into her seat and closed her eyes.

Eighteen months ago, when her hair had still been brown, Scott Parkinson of 'Business Edge,' a highly regarded New York business magazine, had requested an interview. He was writing an article on successful American businesswomen. Although she'd always steered clear of reporters, she thought it would be a fitting end to her long career, so agreed to the interview.

But she'd royally messed up. When published, the article inferred that her success was a mere byproduct of her father's legacy. That her inheritance had been so big it would have taken a complete idiot to screw things up. She'd been furious.

Thinking back, she accepted that her answers had been a little ambiguous and at best, too simplistic.

"Tell me," Scott asked. "To what you owe your success?"

Of course, he was referring to business. He hadn't meant success as a wife, a mother or a decent human being, the things that really mattered. He meant the kind of success measured in dollars. He didn't want to hear about the amount of emotional capital it had cost.

"Determination to carry on my father's legacy of hard work for high gains," she'd said. *What a stupid answer.*

Sylvia had been nine when her mother died. Her father Edward Freeman, land magnet and entrepreneur, had been completely obsessed by business. To most, it was survival. To him, it was a game. If he wasn't running his businesses, he was playing the market, leaving no time for Sylvia or her brother Ian, four years her senior. But the more indifferent he was toward her, the more she pursued his affections.

When Ian turned 16, her father attempted to teach him the business. But Ian wasn't wired that way. A born tree hugger, he was repulsed by his father's underhand and ruthless business tactics. Two years later, after handing Sylvia a note for her father, he swiftly walked out of their lives forever. He left for New Zealand, to study oceanography.

"What are you going to do?" Sylvia asked her father, as she watched him read Ian's letter.

"Nothing." He simply tore up the letter and tossed it into the wastepaper bin. She remembered looking down at the pieces of the letter, thinking that if he could disregard his son so easily, she didn't stand a chance.

With nothing else to do, Sylvia hung around her father's office. At first, he resented the intrusion, but slowly he revealed the intricacies and complexities of running his businesses. By default, she became her father's personal assistant and this was how she acquired her business acumen.

Sylvia opened her eyes and glanced at the financial district on her left. Her need for love and acceptance from her father had been so strong, that success in business was purely incidental. Would Scott have printed that? She didn't think so. But it was the truth.

Her medication made her dozy. The rhythm of the car bouncing over the expansion strips on the Bay Bridge rocked her, luring her eyes closed again.

"Tell me how Freeman Enterprises came to be one of the most prestigious companies in America today," Scott asked.

"Well, where should I start?"

"How about from the time you took over from your father?"

"I was 22 years old when my father died. My brother, who had made New Zealand his home, gave me sole control of the business. There were plenty of predators on the sidelines waiting for me to fuck ..." Scott glanced up. She smiled, "waiting for me to slip up. So it was crucial I trod carefully."

"I spent the first couple of years scrutinizing my father's businesses, particularly his strategic decisions. Almost half of his businesses were associated with the steel industry and he'd done a brilliant job of catching the postwar market in high performance alloys. But times were changing and customers were becoming more sophisticated and specialized. The booming automotive and construction industries wanted their steel piled high and cheap, so we had to get big and keep costs low to stay competitive. In contrast, the arms and aerospace industries needed high quality but smaller quantities. We found ourselves stuck in the middle, too small for the big companies, yet too big and sloppy to turn out a quality product."

"So you sold off most of the steel-related businesses," Scott asked.

"Yes, but we kept the specialty steel and forging businesses and focused on the arms and aerospace markets. However, the end of the Vietnam war signaled the start of a retrenchment and consolidation in our remaining arms related, steel markets. Furthermore, steel itself was becoming displaced by high strength alloys and composites. It became apparent that this side of our business would soon become a liability. So, in quick succession, I offloaded all our interests in steel to our competitors. In turn, the new owners closed them down to reduce capacity and maintain their own margins."

"And how did you feel about the adverse publicity, being accused of being an asset stripper, for instance."

"It was a difficult time, but I had no choice. Computers were beginning to revolutionize supply chain management. Customers were destocking. Mergers and acquisitions were announced daily. I knew that if I wanted to preserve shareholder value and maintain control, I'd have to make some drastic and unpopular changes. Some employees belonged to families that had worked for my father's company for generations and they just expected lifetime employment. The closures were a shock. Understandably, I was hated for it."

"By the end of 1983, Freeman Enterprises had sold 45% of its businesses," Scott reported. "Sylvia Freeman amassed more than $70,000,000 to invest in the overhaul of her land development business. How much the company actually generated from the investment is unclear."

It was true that she acquired a great deal of money selling off the other companies but she'd worked fucking hard during the most turbulent period in business history.

"How did you manage to balance your personal and professional life?" Scott asked.

That threw her. How could she tell him she hadn't had much of a 'personal life?' Her twenties had been spent dodging gold diggers. And throughout she had worked incessantly on building the business. How funny, she thought, that her own life had shadowed her father's even to the end. She'd started out lonely and finished up the same, with a blip in the middle. Jim had been dead for over six years now. And as for Sally, well, she hoped that God would grant her enough time to salvage something there.

"I prefer to keep my personal life, private," she said.

The little prick. Screw the family name. She should have told him the whole story, she thought. He wouldn't have printed it, but getting it off her chest, would've made her feel better and saved a bundle on therapy.

11

It was around 2:00 pm when Sally left Helen's for the grocery store. She felt frazzled by what Joan had told her. The Hammonds were the last people she thought would have marital problems. She lapped the aisles a couple of times before placing a single can of pork and beans into her shopping cart. Then she went down the ice cream aisle again. *Was John having an affair? Was that the real reason he stayed at the apartment so much? That's what Darnell thought. I'd read it on his face.* She felt fragmented, as though the building blocks of her world had been knocked over and put back together differently. *Why the hell do people need so much choice of ice cream? Don't people realize that there's more to life than ice cream!* She opened one of the refrigerator doors, pulled out the first tub of ice cream she put her hands on and tossed it into her cart. Rounding the bottom end of the aisle, she headed back up the canned vegetable aisle. *Screw Darnell.* Agitated, she rapidly tossed more cans of pork and beans into her cart, stopping only when she became aware that she was being watched. Standing beside her, a young woman with a baby glanced in

Sally's cart, then eyed her with suspicion. Sally dropped the can she was holding into her cart and made a hasty retreat to the checkout. As she unloaded her goods onto the conveyor, she counted 19 cans of pork and beans and a single tub of cookie dough ice cream.

Her young, heavily made-up checker, unenthusiastically moved Sally's goods over the barcode sensor. The woman with the baby was now at the next checkout. She said something to her checker and they both looked across at Sally. Thinking they must have recognized her from the news, she flushed and picked up her purse to leave.

"Forty-two dollars and five cents," said her checker.

Sally quickly located her wallet and pulled out $45 in cash while her checker loaded her shopping into plastic bags. *Couldn't she go faster?* Painfully aware that she was still being scrutinized, Sally also began filling bags with her goods. Finally, she loaded her cart, handed over the money and fled the store without waiting for her change or a receipt.

Sally opened her front door and immediately heard laughter from the backyard. She could see Mike, Matt and Andy but a fourth person with gray hair had their back to the window. *Who's that?* She dropped her groceries in the hallway next to a suitcase. *Mom?* She stepped up to the window. Her voice was unmistakable.

"Don't know," her mother said. "I didn't stay around to find out." The builders laughed. Mike laughed so hard he almost fell off his makeshift seat.

Sally had only known her mother as a well-groomed professional with brown, shoulder length hair. *Of course, the chemo.* Now her hair was silvery gray and she wore jeans and a T-shirt, clothes she hadn't seen her wear in years. She felt a pang of jealously as she watched her mother interact so easily with the builders, something she had never managed to do.

Mike spotted her at the window and staggered to his feet. She went out to join them.

"Hi, Mom."

The workmen immediately started clearing up their lunches, making her feel like a party pooper.

"Hello darling." Her mother stood up and gave her a hug. When she drew away, Sally noticed how much older she seemed. Her short cropped, gray hair made her look softer, more approachable, like a trendy grandmother. *If only.*

"You're early!" Sally said.

"Yes, I managed to catch an earlier flight. Wasn't I lucky?"

"You've completely caught me off guard. How was your flight?"

"Uneventful. Which is always good."

There was an awkward silence. Sally racked her brains, trying to think of something else to say. "I'm just about to make coffee. Would you like one?"

"No thank you, darling. Andy's taken good care of me."

Sally raised an eyebrow at him. "Oh, that's nice of him."

"I like the work you've done here. It's fabulous."

"Thanks," Sally replied. Of course, her mother was just making small talk. She could hardly make a valid judgment since she had never seen the house before. "It seems to have taken ages." They both stepped inside. "There was a time when I'd wished we'd never started. But apart from a couple of closets and a little plumbing, it's all done."

"You look well," her mother said.

"Thanks." She was about to ask after her mother's health but then thought better of it.

Her mother finished glancing around the room and turned to face her. Again, an awkward silence stung the air. Sally turned to the kitchen to make herself a drink and caught sight of her mother's luggage.

"Let me show you your room." Sally picked up the suitcase and they headed down the hallway. She opened the door to her old bedroom. "This is ours, but it's more comfortable. John and I will sleep in the spare."

"Oh, you don't have to do that!"

"I insist. We'll be perfectly happy in the front bedroom." She dropped the case on the bed and they returned to the living room. Sally retrieved her shopping from the hallway and heaved the bags onto the kitchen counter.

Her mother parked herself against the stove, and faced the kitchen sink window. "So, what's new with you and John?"

"Nothing much. As always, John is working outrageously long hours." She opened the freezer compartment and tossed the tub of ice cream into it. "and I've been working on the front garden," she said, closing the door. "I'd expected to be landscaping the back by now, but as you can see it's still a barren wasteland out there. She turned around, opened the cupboard directly above her and started stacking the cans inside. "And I guess the workmen told you about last night."

"Last night? No, what about last night?"

"Well. There's been a bit of vandalism in the area." Sally said.

"Oh, dear. What's happened?"

"Some kids, the police think, have been shooting out windows in the neighborhood. And we were hit last night," she explained.

"Shootings! Here?"

Sally felt her face heat up, instantly regretting she'd said anything about it.

"Oh, my God!"

"Mom, it's not as bad as it sounds. As I said, the police think it's just high school kids," she said, as calmly as possible, but inside she was really wound up.

"Someone shot at the house! Were you inside!"

Sally slammed the cupboard door shut. "Mom, please don't overreact! Everything's fine now! John thinks it's really nothing to get upset about!"

Her mother drew closer. "I'm sorry. It's just so shocking! So that's what Mike meant about the cavalry showing up."

"What? Oh, yes. But everything's fine now mom. Really."

"Sally, if you need help. If either you or …" her mother sighed, "John … need help. I'm here for you, OK? I know you think I'm an interfering bitch, but I'm not going to risk spoiling this week, by poking my nose where it's not wanted."

"Thanks mom." She bundled up the empty plastic bags and stuffed them into the recycling bin underneath the sink, surprised and relieved that her mother had dropped the matter.

"It's a lovely day," her mother said. "Why don't we go do something?"

"Like what?"

"Oh, I don't know?" Her mother glanced through the window. "Why don't we go visit a garden center, buy some plants for the backyard?"

She looked into her mother's eyes, realizing that it wasn't just the gray hair that had softened her.

"Mom that would be great."

12

The two women returned from the garden center. They opened the back doors of Sally's Volkswagen sedan and plucked plants from the foot-wells.

"These are lovely mom," Sally said. They shut the doors and headed inside the house. "Thank you."

"You're very welcome," she replied.

Sally slid open the patio door and placed them in the backyard. "It's getting near dinnertime. Maybe I'll get a chance to plant them tomorrow. Fancy a cup of tea?"

"I thought you'd never ask. I'll get the rest of the plants."

Out front, Sylvia opened the trunk of the car and pulled out a box containing pansies, cyclamens and daisies, congratulating herself on a successful afternoon. By chance, suggesting a trip to the garden center seemed to be exactly the right thing to do. She couldn't remember a time when Sally had opened up so much. She chatted about Californian native plants and her love for gardening. She even mentioned her father, something she hadn't done to any extent, for years.

Sylvia shut the trunk, leant against the side of the car, closed her eyes and faced the sun. God it feels good. Yes, she agreed with Sally, Jim would've loved California. Then her thoughts returned to the one thing that had been bugging her all afternoon - the shooting. Like Sally, she thought it was probably some local vandals with nothing else better to do, but even so, it was a loose end and she couldn't let it rest there. But afraid of ruining the afternoon, she hadn't pursued the matter. She would just have to do her own digging. Sylvia entered the house, closed the door behind her and placed the plants with the others.

The telephone rang. Sally picked up the receiver. "Oh, hello Mrs. Davies. Yes, it is. No, No, I'm fine. Oh, we have?" She turned and glanced at the kitchen clock. It read 3:12 pm. Sylvia glanced at her watch and noted that it was 5:10 pm.

"Oh OK. Yes, I will. Thank you for letting me know. Bye." Sally replaced the receiver and went to the microwave. "That was one of my neighbors," she said, glancing at her watch, then altering the LED clock on the microwave. "We've had a power outage. Apparently, it's been on and off all afternoon."

"Oh, what a drag." Sylvia made herself comfortable on the couch, shaking off her shoes and lifting her feet onto it.

"You can say that again. We've had more than a few brownouts this summer and I suspect it'll only get worse when the new housing development's built." Sally altered the kitchen clock above the cooker then went back to the telephone. "I'd better listen to these messages." She pressed the button flashing on the answering machine.

"Sally, it's Joe. Would you please wire the final payment to my account at Bank of the West." He left details of the amount and his account number.

"In your dreams. Not until Andy's finished the closets," Sally vented. "You wouldn't believe how much that guy has messed us around." The next few calls were from reporters requesting interviews. She fast-forwarded through them all.

"This is a message for Mrs. Pringle. My name is Sam Myers. I'm chairman of the local neighborhood watch committee. We're holding a meeting tonight at eight o'clock at the Presbyterian Church to discuss the increase of crime in the area and in particular, the recent shootings. I'm calling to invite you to come along. Our aim is to set up a special committee to put pressure on the police to clear up the situation as soon as possible. We hope to see you there. Bye."

The machine continued playing more messages from the press.

"I don't like the sound of a special committee," Sally said. "Sounds a bit radical. Don't you think?"

"I think you should go. You don't have to participate in anything. Just tell them what the police have told you. And you never know, you might find out a thing or two yourself."

"Yes, I guess you're right. But what about you? It's your first night here."

"Oh, I'll be fine. You go to your meeting. I'm probably going to have an early night anyway."

"Well, if you're sure?"

"I'll be fine Sally, really."

"Hi Sally, it's ..." said a voice. Then the message suddenly stopped. The power had cut out again.

"Oh, here we go again!" Sally said.

"What shall we do for dinner? Shall we eat out?" Sylvia asked.

"We could. But I have enough in the refrigerator to fix us a salad."

"Good idea. Besides, the restaurants might not be operating."

As they started to eat dinner, the power came back on. Sally chatted about Fenton. Sylvia got the impression that she had really settled into life here. She spoke affectionately about her friends and particularly about Helen Pearce, who seemed her closest.

Sylvia's alarm sounded on her watch. She pulled out the small pill container from the pocket of her shorts, flipped it open, and swallowed two blue pills. "And does John like Fenton?" she asked, closing the container and slipping it back into her shorts.

Sally fired her a quick, sharp glance. "Oh, he's getting used to it. The remodel has been much slower than we anticipated and he's been extremely irritated by it all. I can't blame him, so have I." She got up and cleared the table. "And he finds suburban life a little too quiet. You know, before we moved here, I hadn't realized John had always lived in large cities." She opened the dishwasher and placed the plates in the rack. "He thinks San Francisco is small, never mind living out here. I guess it takes a bit of getting used to." She came back to collect the condiments and glanced at her watch before picking them up from the table. "Oh, it's almost eight o'clock, I'd better get going."

Sylvia looked at her own watch, it was only 7:40 pm. The church, which Sally had pointed out on their way back from the garden center, was only a couple of blocks away. She suspected that Sally was derailing any further conversation about John. She was dying to ask, in not so many words, why the son of a bitch wasn't home, particularly after the events of the night before.

Sylvia got up and stacked the place mats. "I'll clear the rest away. You get off to your meeting," she said, shooing her away from the table.

Sally promptly picked up her keys, said goodbye and left.

After starting the dishwasher, Sylvia looked around for something to occupy her mind. Spotting the entertainment center behind the couch, she went over and filtered through the music. She picked out a classical compilation CD and slotted it into the player. Elgar's 'Nimrod' trickled soothingly through the speakers, immediately making her feel relaxed. Above her was a bookshelf filled with paperbacks. One entitled 'European Stories' caught her eye. From the back cover she read, "An adventure in Europe covering places off the beaten track. Meet the people and see the landscape …" The fleeting memory of Jim, running along the platform at London's Euston Station as her train pulled away, suddenly sprang to mind. She glanced affectionately at her wedding ring. What a mess she'd been before they'd met.

Shortly after her 28th birthday, she'd received a letter from her brother informing her that he and his girlfriend of five years were expecting a baby and were getting married. Up to

125

that point, she'd let her personal life bumble along, but this news came as a wakeup call. She realized that almost everyone she knew was married or had a significant other to share their lives. While she, on the other hand, had no-one. She felt that unless she found a man from a different planet, she would never find a suitable husband. No longer able to suppress her loneliness, she had what she construed as an epiphany, and what others described as a nervous breakdown.

It happened not long after she'd received her brother's letter, as she sat in a board meeting. She was dreadfully tired, because she hadn't slept properly for weeks. Business being second nature, she vaguely listened to the account of the state of the company. What was the point of all this, she thought, if she didn't have anyone to share it with?

"Slazenger's strategic plan is to discover future development around ..." said Gerald, *married, three kids and a fourth on the way.*

She tried her best to concentrate on Gerald's presentation but her sight became fuzzy and unfocused, making her feel sick and dizzy. Gerald's voice sounded a long way off. She blinked a few times and for a moment both her vision and hearing returned.

"Solomon Mackenzie, in its fifth year expects ..." Gerald continued.

Again, her vision and hearing became impaired. She wondered whether she was having a migraine. She looked beyond the boardroom table and realized she was able to focus further away. A picture on the opposite wall caught her eye and thankfully, stopped the room from spinning. The brightly colored oil painting was a peaceful scene of a valley with a small quaint village. It had been in the boardroom for the past five years but until that point, she hadn't given it a second glance. But now it captivated her. Sylvia ached for its quietness, its stillness. She suddenly realized what she needed to do.

"That's it!" She blurted. Her focus returned to the boardroom table like a bolt of lightning. The board members were glaring at her.

"As I was just saying, ..." Gerald continued.

"Yes." Sylvia said, dismissively. "I agree it's the way to go, Gerald."

"But I haven't mentioned..."

She raised her hand stopping Gerald in his tracks "I have every confidence that you and the board will make the right decision," she said, smiling. She gathered up her papers and set them to one side. "Yes, what a wonderful team we are. Don't you think?"

The board members seemed dumbfounded.

"And it's such a wonderful day. Don't you think? What kind of day do you think it is, Bill?" she asked.

"Err ..."

"Yes, Bill, four children, two grandchildren. What do you think?", she asked, glancing through the window.

Bill turned to the window. "The weather?" he asked, like it was a trick question.

Sylvia nodded.

Everyone stared at the CFO with trepidation. Predictably Bill took the middle approach. "Nice! Yes, I believe it's a nice day," he stammered, "for the time of year, of course," he added cautiously.

"Yes, and I think so, too! Well, unless there is anything else to discuss?"

Gerald attempted to speak, but she put up her hand and silenced him. "I have an announcement to make."

The board members stared at her like she had just sprouted another head.

"I'm going to take some time off. A vacation!" she said, smiling excitedly.

Some gasped, some swallowed hard. But all stared at her with frozen anxiety. You could have heard a pin drop.

"A long ... vacation. Starting right now!" she added briskly.

The board members muttered amongst themselves. Gerald dabbed his brow with a handkerchief.

"Now Gerald, I'm leaving you in charge," she said, rising from her seat. "Try not to bankrupt the company while I'm away," she teased. He laughed nervously.

"Meeting's over. Off you go!" she said, shooing them away.

Slowly, they gathered their agendas, stuffed them into their briefcases and silently filed out of the room as though they were in a funeral procession.

Sylvia strolled over to the painting. Anna, her secretary, peered around the door. "Is everything alright, Miss Freeman?"

"Yes Anna, everything's fine."

After the board meeting, it was rumored that many of the board members had immediately started networking, convinced that the company was about to be sold from underneath them.

Sylvia took the painting off the wall and placed it on the boardroom table. The village, she noted, was on one side, and a meadow was on the other. A stone bridge over a river linked the two. A young boy sat on it, fishing. She recalled seeing the painting in her father's home office but had no idea when or how it had got to the boardroom. She had once asked her father about the painting and he'd told her that the village was in Scotland, where he believed his grandfather had lived as a child. She turned it over and tore off the back panel. There she saw written on the back of the canvas, 'Durisdeer, Scotland, 1890.' She wasn't interested in discovering her roots. The less she knew about her father's side of the family, the better. She merely wanted to get away and figured Scotland was as good a place as anywhere.

She pressed Anna's extension number on the telephone console. "Anna, please book me a flight to London."

"Leaving when Miss Freeman?"

"Tomorrow, the earliest you can get," She replied.

"Returning when?"

"Don't worry about that. One way will do for now."

Sylvia recalled her excitement as her plane touched down at Heathrow. Of course she'd traveled to London many times but always on business. She believed the reason she hadn't met any 'down to earth' men was the fact that she lived a privileged life. So she decided to travel as most people did, on public transport. She had no plans, didn't know what was ahead of her and had no chauffeur to deliver her safely to a hotel. Deciding she was in no rush to get to

Scotland, she boarded the 9:45 am train from Euston to Manchester, with the intention of staying a week in the Lake District. It had already been a new experience navigating her way to the station on the underground.

As the train pulled out of the station, she noticed a tall, dark-haired man, wearing a backpack, running alongside. He smiled and waved at her, finally jumping onto the train just before the platform disappeared. He opened the door of her carriage and flopped down opposite her, sweating and breathing profusely.

"That was close!" he said, panting. He slung his backpack onto the seat beside him. He was extremely thin and grubby. His name, he told her was Jim Campbell, and he was on his way home to Manchester after hiking the Pyrenees. Later, she learned, that his skinniness was due to him getting lost in the Mountains. She told him that she admired his spirit and in her own way, was going on a little adventure of her own. On route, he taught her to play poker and told her about his trip.

"You know I've been rattling on all this time," he said. "I don't know a thing about you."

"Well, there's not much to tell," Sylvia said warily. She'd always avoided telling people she met socially, particularly men, what she did because she'd see that opportunist glint in their eyes. Jim waited for her to continue. What the hell, she thought, she'd probably never see him again.

Sylvia chuckled now when she thought how wrong she'd been.

"Well among other things, I own a property development company."

"Oh, and do ya like it?"

That floored her. She hadn't been asked that before and never really considered whether she liked it. It was just something she did. "Yes, I think so."

"You think so! You mean you don't know? I'd never do anything I didn't like doing. I mean you spend a lot of time at work, don't ya? Life's too bloody short. And you can't take money with ya, can ya?"

She smiled. "No, you can't. What do you do?"

"Nothing. I used to work in a steel plant. Then one day I thought, fuck this for a lark, I'm off."

"So what did you do?"

"I took me savings and decided to go on a quest. Find out what it's all about. You know what I mean?"

"Yes," she said, thoughtfully. "Yes, I think I do. Did you come up with any answers?"

"No. But I had a bloody good time trying to find out," he laughed. "What are you doing in Blighty, anyway?"

Sylvia frowned, not knowing what he meant.

"The UK!"

"Well, I guess the same as you, really. I just wanted to get away. You know, drop off the map for a while."

"Yeah. I know exactly what you mean. I had a great time. Clears the head," he said, tapping his temple with a forefinger.

She smiled. "What are you going to do now?"

"Back to the plant, I suppose. Make some more money."

"Then what?"

He didn't answer. Just shrugged his shoulders, like he hadn't a care in the world. "Want another game?"

Sally's phone rang, propelling Sylvia back to the present. She let the answering machine pick it up. Her body tensed when she heard John's arrogant voice.

"Sally, it's John. Sorry for not calling earlier. I just got caught up in the chaos here. There's a problem, I can't explain over the phone but I'm going to have to stay in the city tonight, so I can get an early start tomorrow. I'll try to call you later. Bye."

John was the only person she knew who could make an apology sound like an insult. He made her skin crawl. *What a slimeball.* She opened the book and slowly drifted over to the couch as she read the introduction "Thor's Cave – The Peak District. You might well ask why my first chapter starts in the middle of England ..."

The lights went out and the music suddenly stopped. *Another outage.* She snapped the book shut, deciding that she would get an early night. The medication had made her drowsy and she would sleep like a baby. She felt her way into the bedroom and automatically switched on the light. *Duh*, she said to herself. She undressed, slipped on the nightgown she had laid out earlier, and got into bed.

The moonlight shone through the curtains and settled on a couple of framed photographs placed on the bedside table. One was of Jim, and the other, a wedding photograph of John and Sally.

She remembered having John checked out when Sally first started dating him. He'd come up clean, far too squeaky for Sylvia's liking. Straight A's at school, rowing team at Boston

University, an MBA from Harvard. No police record, not even a parking ticket.

On meeting him, John was all that she'd expected. A socially crippled, boring, ego-driven individual, with no other conversation than business and an obvious thirst for money. Not the kind of husband she had hoped for Sally.

Sally asked her what she thought of him. Sylvia told her that he seemed OK, but maybe she should keep her options open and date other men as well. Of course, Sally had seen right through that. Maybe it had been Sylvia's tone of voice or perhaps her body language, but the result had been an even frostier relationship between them.

Sylvia turned over to her other side, feeling partly responsible for her marrying John. She suspected that Sally had deepened her relationship with him to spite her. Handled differently, the relationship may well have fizzled out a long time ago. She tried to recall when it had started to go wrong between them. Even when Sally was a child they'd been at each other's throats.

Determined to bring her up as normal as possible, Sally had attended public school. Sylvia encouraged her to play with kids of a lower class and from different races. At the age of 12, Sylvia became aware that she was having problems at school and suspected an attention deficit disorder.

She consulted Dr. Elgin, an educational psychologist and a close friend of Gerald's. The doctor had been retired a couple of years, but agreed to give her his opinion. After a two hour evaluation, he told Sylvia that in his opinion Sally's problem was not chemical, but related to her home environment. Cutting to the chase, he'd said that Sally lacked parental discipline and guidance. As Jim was Sally's main caregiver, she discussed the problem with him. Jim told her he thought Dr. Elgin was off his head and that she shouldn't have approached a 'quack' in the first place.

Once pointed out, Sylvia could clearly see that the doctor's evaluation had been right. Sally's inability to finish anything, and her overly carefree attitude, was also one of Jim's traits. She thought it ironic that her husband's carefree attitude, which she had found so appealing and necessary for her own sanity, had such a negative impact on their daughter.

Sylvia tried to enforce rules and set boundaries. Homework first, play later she'd insist. But as soon as her back was turned, the rules would go out of the window. If there had been any friction between Jim and herself it was over Sally's upbringing. She resented being the bad cop, while he got all the affection and respect. However, she believed it was her parental duty to raise Sally the best she could, even if it made her unpopular.

On Sally's 18th birthday, she attempted to rekindle their relationship by offering to buy her a car of her choice. Sally was ecstatic and chose a red BMW convertible. But before the month was out, she left a message with Celia, the housekeeper, asking her mother to swap it for a Porsche. Sylvia was livid. She thought Sally unsalvageable; that she had become a spoiled and ungrateful brat.

However, with the onset of cancer, Sylvia had plenty of time to think back over her life and the decisions she'd made. She realized that her decision to keep Sally out of her life, had more to do with her own feelings as a failed parent, than anything Sally had done.

Sylvia turned over again. Was she crazy to think that she could make it up to her after all these years, especially with so little time left? She leaned over the bed and felt on the floor for her shorts. She pulled out her pill case and flipped it open. And for the first time, swallowed another one of her pills.

13

Tony had been waiting patiently by the back door for the past 20 minutes, pleased that his target hadn't taken flight. The drapes were drawn, and he'd heard music coming from the living room. He deduced that his cover from the night before had not been blown. At the very least, he expected police surveillance, if the authorities had the slightest doubt that the shooting was something other than a high school prank. Even so, his fuck up made him edgy, and instead of waiting until tomorrow to leave the country, he intended to leave as soon as he could. He checked his watch. If he got lucky, he could catch the 10:32 pm flight to Heathrow, then a connecting flight the next morning to Athens. A change of clothes, a new identity, and a small suitcase awaited him in his car, parked only a few blocks away. All he needed to do was get this job done, call in the drop and he was on his way. You could call it plan C, but in truth Tony was winging it.

Fortunately, it seemed his target had turned in early. The music had been switched off and the house was now in total darkness. Dressed in black, wearing a ski mask and surfing boots, Tony eased a thin piece of metal down the inside of the patio door lock and slid it open. Listening intently, he crept slowly and lightly across the living room floor. Other than the humming of the refrigerator, the house was silent. He stepped into the bedroom hallway and noticed that one of the bedroom doors was slightly ajar. He pushed it wider, extending his arm full length, then crept inside. The familiar surge of adrenaline shot through his veins, as he spotted the outline of his victim in bed. He bent over her. A wisp of warm breath brushed his face. He reached over to the other side of the bed and picked up a pillow. Placing it over her face, he pressed down as hard as he could. She gave out a muffled groan. Her hands gripped his wrists. She writhed wildly about, kicking like a mule. To keep control, he straddled her and pressed down even harder. Then the lights came on. *What the fuck?* Tony glanced over his shoulder, releasing some pressure from the pillow. His victim managed to slip from underneath it, to one side. She screamed and poked his eyes with her fingers.

"Arrgh, fuck," he yelled, closing his eyes in pain but managing to grasp one of her arms.

"Help! Someone help me!" she screamed.

He rubbed his eyes with his free hand while firmly holding onto her with the other. She punched his face, but he still held fast. She bit his arm. *Fuck!* He let go. The bed bounced, then he heard a thud; she had slipped to the floor. Again, she yelled for help.

Tony shook his head. His eyes were blurred but he could see the pink outline of her. He pounced on her. She kicked, screamed and lashed out with her hands, pulling his hair and punching his face. He had to shut her up. He located her throat and locked his hands around it. She grasped his hands, trying to pry them off. Suddenly she stopped screaming. He tightened his grip even further, initiating the familiar gurgling sounds of death. Then his eyes cleared. *Shit! Who the fuck is this?* This was not his target. This woman was much older. Her silvery, gray hair reminded him of his mother. She'd even had similar brown eyes and for a moment she became his mother. Taken aback, he loosened his grip a little. He felt her windpipe re-inflate beneath his fingers.

This wasn't his mother or the woman he'd been hired to kill. Nonetheless, he'd have to kill her now. Again, he gripped her throat tightly. Surprisingly, she pushed her throat forward helping him to get a better fix on her throat. She also released her hands from his wrists and became limp, well before he had exerted deadly pressure. Tony looked into her eyes. She was calm and steadfast. Her whole demeanor seemed resigned to her fate. A second time, his mom flashed through his mind. He closed his eyes, trying to block the woman and his mother out. He started to pant. Pushing his arms straight, he tried to squeeze harder but his fingers felt numb, as though he were gripping a cold metal pipe. His breaths became spare and shallow, little air reached his lungs. Suddenly, a sharp pain struck his chest. He felt as though a giant hand inside him had squeezed all the air from his lungs. He tried to take a deep breath, but his lungs remained flat, the pain stabbing him again, this time much harder. He released the woman, rolled off her onto the floor

138

clutching his chest. He could hear the woman, wheezing, coughing, gasping for air.

"Come on then, you bastard," she said between gasps, "get it over with."

Tearing pain ripped across Tony's chest like a chainsaw. His head tightened, he knew he was close to passing out.

He desperately needed his inhaler. He pried one of his hands from his chest to his pants. Frantically, he searched for the opening of his pocket, but was unable to find it. Cold and clammy, sweat seeped from him. Losing all his energy, his arm dropped to the floor. He lay completely still, staring across the cream carpet to the wall. All he could hear was the slow, labored pumping of his heart. In a moment, he knew it would stop altogether.

He saw feet and then the woman's face. She yelled something at him, but he couldn't hear, he could only see. He thought inhaler, but couldn't mouth the words. Then, he saw her rear and felt a tug on his pants. A second later the woman's face returned to his. She pulled off his ski mask and forced his mouth open. He then felt a long, slow slither of wet, cold air wind its way down his throat, windpipe and finally his lungs. He coughed, spluttered and finally his lungs sucked in some air.

"Breathe, breathe, that's it," the woman said. Tony grasped the hand holding the inhaler and again she sprayed into his mouth. He coughed again and managed to take deeper breaths. He felt the blood rush back to his brain. It made him feel dizzy, but the tightness in his head dissipated.

"You need to sit up." The woman helped lift his shoulders off the floor. He sat up, brought his knees to his chin and hung his head between his legs. The woman suddenly scuttled backward against the wall.

"Oh Christ," Tony gasped, "I nearly died."

"Yes, so did I," snapped the woman, rubbing her neck. He looked sideways at her. She glanced at the telephone, then back at him.

"It's OK lady," he said, breathlessly. "I'm done....... I'm in no state to do anything now."

Tony staggered to his feet. Turning to her, he raised a hand in thanks. He felt like shit. He ached all over and he'd messed up again. He wasn't about to analyze how he'd fucked up this time, he'd stared death straight in the face and he was outta there.

"Wait," the woman said.

He held onto the edge of the door and turned to face her. She was on her feet.

"What are you doing here?" Her eyes were steely, her face taught. She was well pumped. "What's this about?"

Screw this. He turned away and started through the door.

"Oh, no you don't." The woman ran in front of him. She pushed him away from the door and pinned him against the wall. "Why were you in my daughter's house?"

Even though Tony had somewhat recovered from his ordeal he still felt compromised by his asthma attack and the woman had caught him off-guard. There weren't many people who'd try to tackle their assailant, especially when they had the chance to get away.

"You thought I was my daughter, didn't you?"

He pushed her away. "Just your typical burglary, that's all," he said, panting.

"Oh? Yeah. So what were you after? Eh? Show me what you've got!"

He desperately needed a rest. "Look, you're alive. Be grateful will ya?" he said, once again moving to the doorway. She suddenly grabbed his balls. Already sore, he bent over in agony and looked up at the woman's contorted face. He could see and feel she was putting a lot of effort into her grip. He felt the bruised blood rush from his gonads, around his body, dispersing pain wherever it traveled.

"Now listen to me, you piece of shit. You're going to tell me what's going on, she yelled. "Now!" she tightened her grip even more.

"Lady," he whimpered. But he could see she was not going to budge. Cold sweat ran down his forehead into his eyes. He felt like throwing up. "OK," he mouthed.

To his relief, she let go and backed away. He sighed and fell face down onto the bed, winded. He turned his head sideways. "OK! OK!" he sighed breathlessly. "I was hired to kill Sally Pringle." Tony flinched as he felt the blood rush back to his southern regions. He put his hands underneath him and cupped his genitals.

"Oh God!" She sat down on the bed making it bounce.

Tony winced at the sudden movement. He thought briefly of the babies he might never have.

"Nothing personal. It's my job," he gasped.

"But who for? Why?"

"I don't know! I never know."

"Was it a man or a woman who hired you?" she asked.

"I have no idea. I never speak to the source. I have an agent, a go-between."

He turned onto his side then slowly pushed himself off the bed. He held onto the door a moment, recovering his breath, and glanced back at the woman. She looked shell-shocked. He felt a stab of sympathy, but mostly she intrigued him.

"When I was strangling you, you went limp," he said, suddenly voicing what had been bugging him.

She looked up at him dazed.

He nodded over to the floor. "You stopped fighting and went limp before you should."

"I've got cancer," she said, indifferently. "I've got about four months to live. You were actually doing me a favor."

"Oh … Sorry, he said genuinely. Tony had little fear of death, except for dying slowly and painfully. In this respect he could totally empathize with her. "I don't suppose …" He lifted up his hands.

"No," she shook her head. "Not now. Do you think it's her husband?"

"What? Lady, I told you. I don't know and I don't care." He spotted a wedding photograph of a couple on the bedside table. The woman looked like his target. She was smiling, he had a conceited expression on his face. "That them?"

She turned to the photograph. "Yes," she said.

"He looks a bit of a dickhead."

"Yes, he is. Don't suppose you feel like another job, do you?' she said, jokingly. Suddenly, her face brightened.

"Oh, no, no. No lady. Hey, I'm retiring. I've retired. This is… was my last job."

The woman started crying. "It's just, well, I feel such a failure. I've been such a rotten mother. And now that she really needs me, I won't be here. And she deserves better than that asshole!" she said sharply, glancing at the photograph. She covered her face with her hands and sobbed, her shoulders bouncing up and down.

He willed himself to move, to leave. The woman's sobs were pitiful. Her whole body shook with hopelessness. Again, he thought of his mother. On her deathbed, her last thoughts were for Tony, and her sadness for having to leave him alone in the world, without anyone to love or care for him. He supposed the woman felt the same about her daughter.

"Damn," he said, plopping himself beside her. "Stop crying."

She leaned against him. Awkwardly, he placed an arm around her.

"Look," she said, pulling herself away from him. "If you help me find out who's behind this. I'll pay you anything you want."

Desperation was written on her face. He had seen it many times before; on the faces of victims he was about to kill. But nevertheless, he'd killed them. But this woman had saved his life. And for some odd reason, Mary's face popped into his head. And as much as he wanted to tell the woman to go screw herself, he couldn't. Something was niggling him and he had to get to the bottom of it. "OK! OK! I guess I have some unfinished business myself," he said, grabbing the picture frame from the bedside table and ripping out the photograph.

14

Tony woke the next morning feeling extremely agitated. Besides battered and bruised, he was still in his shitty little apartment in Ashwood and not somewhere exotic.

He stared at the naked light bulb, dangling from the tar-stained ceiling above his head, wrapped in a cloak of cobwebs. *What the hell I am still doing here? Last night, I almost murdered the wrong woman and nearly damn well died myself.* He went over each humiliating moment and concluded that his impatience and frustration had been his downfall. But whatever the reason, he'd let his emotions get the better of him. *It's over pal,* he said to himself. He had to get out of the business, now. He'd seen so many colleagues go down, because they hadn't recognized they were past it. And he wasn't about to join them in prison or the cemetery. He would leave on the 11:00 am flight as originally planned and find a job as soon as he could. He had connections, so it wouldn't be difficult. As to the woman, Sylvia, she'd just have to hire some other guy to do her dirty work. And Mary, well, he knew in the cold light of day, it wouldn't work. It was futile to even go there.

He threw off his threadbare sheets and, butt naked, strutted across the floor of his one roomed apartment. After entering his small, damp, mildewed bathroom, he turned on the shower and waited for the water to appear. Arms above his head, he stretched himself awake in front of the bathroom mirror, twisting side to side, examining his upper body. The pipes banged noisily against the back of the sporadically tiled shower wall, as the water unenthusiastically made its way to his bathroom. It appeared in short, sharp intervals and then with such force that two tiles sprang from the wall. He picked up the broken pieces of tile and tossed them into the waste-bin on top of some others. Knowing it was futile to wait for hot water, he stepped into the tub and squeezed the remains of his 'Wash and Go' shampoo onto his head, and then vigorously washed himself under the cold water as the suds slid down his body. He rinsed, turned off the shower, and briskly dried himself.

With the towel folded tightly around his waist, he returned to his bedroom. From the inside of his leather jacket, he plucked out his airline ticket and his cell phone.

"Hello," said a voice. Tony had inadvertently pressed the talk button as he picked up his phone. He placed it against his ear.

"Hello … Hello, David?" He immediately recognized Mary's voice. She could have cursed him and she would still have turned him on.

"Hi," he replied.

"David, it's Mary, from the clinic."

Tony slowly made his way back to his bed. Although flattered she'd called, she was the last person he'd wanted to hear from, just as he was about to leave the country for good.

"Mary Bruin?" she said. "I think, I must have the wrong number."

"No, no, Mary." He sat down on the bed. "This is David."

"Hi..... Well, I was calling to say how much I enjoyed talking to you yesterday and wondered whether we could get together sometime and talk more about the security business."

He wondered whether she was lying in bed. He imagined her scantily dressed in a black lacy top but then again she could be naked. *Oh God!* He stared at the ticket in his hand. *Cut her off. Press the off button.* Then he remembered her from the day before. Her white see-through blouse and her long, fine legs as she glided across the floor.

"But I understand if you're too busy," she said.

"How about lunch," he said. *You dick!* he cursed himself for his moment of weakness.

"Today? I didn't expect ...Well, I get off at noon. What time is good for you? she asked.

Half excited and half disappointed, he tore up his non-refundable plane ticket. "Can you get to Gepettos in Ashwood by 12:30 pm?"

"Yes, I can make that. Oh, and David. Thank you."

———————————

Tony was already seated in a booth in the Italian restaurant when Mary arrived. His heart missed a beat when he spotted her. Not only because she was dressed in her police officer's uniform but because she looked cute in it, in a perverse sort of way.

"Hi," she said, slipping into the seat across from him. She wasn't wearing her protective vest. *Definitely against protocol.*

"Good to see you."

The waitress took their order. Mary chose a pizza.

"I'll have the house salad," he ordered. They handed their menus back to the waitress and she promptly withdrew.

"Are you on your lunch break?" he asked, eyeing her uniform.

"No, I'm off duty. I didn't have time to change."

Mary looked as good as he remembered. Her blonde hair was tied back from her face and her wide, dark green eyes glistened with excitement. Her enthusiasm was contagious. Totally smitten, Tony was unable to stop grinning.

"I'm so glad we could meet," she said. "I've been thinking more about working in security since our conversation yesterday."

"Glad to help. But you know, it's not exactly the most exciting job in the world."

She leaned forward, elbows on the table, chin on her fists, anticipating a lecture. He wondered what the catch was. *This is just too perfect.*

"Well, they're jobs connected with private security agencies," he said adlibbing. "Working at museums, retail stores, airports, armored and industrial security."

"So what field of security do you work?"

"I'm in the private sector."

"Doing what specifically?" she asked.

"I'm a bodyguard."

"Oh!" She seemed animated. "Who do you work for?"

Tony leaned over the table toward her. "If I told you that, I would have to kill ya," he jested.

Mary smiled politely. As expected, his flippant remark cut short any further questioning regarding his fictitious occupation.

The waitress returned with water, cutlery, plates and a breadbasket.

"Yesterday, you said something about being disillusioned with the police force."

She picked up a piece of bread and a carton of butter and placed them on her plate. "Yes. I'm beginning to think that maybe I'm not cut out for it." She peeled back the seal from the butter.

"Oh, why's that?"

"I thought that police work would be exciting, you know, a rush, catching criminals, putting the world to rights," she explained, while buttering her bread.

"Making the world a better place?" he joked.

She laughed. "Yes, I know it sounds corny. I just took it for granted that I'd be good at it."

He frowned not getting her drift. "How come?"

"Well, my father's an ex-chief of police."

"Really." Tony stiffened. To conceal his anxiety, he also placed some bread on his side plate.

"Dad warned me that police work is a brutal environment. I thought I could hack it, but now I'm not so sure."

149

Ex-Police Chief! Now, this is looking decisively bad. She's probably Daddy's little fascist brat. I knew there'd be a catch.

Unsettled by this latest revelation he tried to peel the top off his butter, but his mind was too pre-occupied to handle such a dexterous task. *How could this stunningly beautiful, soft spoken woman be the product of some ex-chief of police for Christ's sake?*

"Here, let me," she said. He handed over the carton and studied her face as she continued talking. "And it's still very much a man's world. They don't take female officers seriously." She opened the butter and handed it back to him.

Mary leaned over the table. He gazed longingly at the deep valley between her breasts. *Don't do that. She'll think you're a pervert.*

"Sometimes, I think I'm on the wrong side of the law," she said, lowering her voice.

Intrigued, he leaned towards her. "Oh, and what makes you think that?"

"Well," she said, glancing furtively over her shoulder, then moving even closer "Cops aren't as straight as you think ..." she whispered.

Mary proceeded to tell him about some scams a couple of her colleagues were involved in. He sympathized with a sigh and a nod here and there, but now that he could peek down her shirt without her noticing, he took full advantage. The top of her breasts looked hard, smooth and shiny. He felt a strong urge to nuzzle his nose between them. Her breath, as she spoke, stroked his ear, making the hairs all over his body tingle.

"What do you think about that," she said, suddenly sitting back.

Tony hadn't heard a word. "What …what do you think about that?" he asked, fumbling for a reply.

"Well, I think they're completely corrupt. You wouldn't believe the things that go down. I joined the force to help society, but if the law's just as corrupt? How can I do my job with a clear conscience?"

Was she for real? He threw his head back and laughed.

She reddened. "A little naïve, I guess, huh?"

"Yes. Just a little," he nodded.

"I think I should go," she said, suddenly springing to her feet.

Instinctively, Tony grabbed her arm. He couldn't let her go, not yet. He hated loose ends and he definitely needed closure here. "No, don't go, I'm sorry. I didn't mean to upset you."

She glanced at his hand on her arm then searched his eyes, as though deciding whether he could be trusted with her feelings.

"Please," he said. The waitress brought their food. To his relief, Mary slowly sat down.

The waitress placed their orders on the table and then disappeared. "I'm sorry, Mary. I didn't realize how bad you felt."

There were tears in her eyes. "It's OK. It's just been a really tough week." She fiddled with a piece of hair that had fallen loose. "The other officers never seem to let up. And yet again, I've been passed over for promotion."

151

"I think you're being too hard on yourself." Tony bit into his bread.

Mary shook her head. "What? How would you know?"

"You just told me."

"I did?" she said.

"In my experience, people say more about themselves with what they don't say than with what they do," he explained. "You said, 'I've been passed over for promotion.' You said it with so little passion. Kinda beaten down, like you really expected it."

"Reality," he continued, loading up his fork with salad. "Is only a state of mind. If you think you didn't deserve that promotion, then you'll believe it and won't get it. You have sole control over your mind and feelings. You really have to be more positive about yourself Mary."

He chewed slowly on a piece of lettuce leaf, allowing what he'd said to sink in.

"Oh Yeah! Well I can't think of one damned reason why I should be? I never get the breaks. I have no control over whether I get promoted." She picked up a piece of pizza and bit sharply into it.

"It's not only the end product that you have to keep your eye on. The way you perceive and the way you are perceived are equally important," he replied.

Tony noticed a couple sitting opposite them. The woman he figured was in her mid-thirties. She had brown, shoulder length hair and wore a cream short sleeved, see-through shirt and a black miniskirt. Her black heels were far too high for an executive or for a high profile office worker. Sitting across from her was a much younger man. He wore a dark blue suit and had short, dark brown hair.

Tony bent over the table towards Mary. "You see that couple over there?" He nodded in the couples direction. She looked over at them. "Tell me, what do you see?" he asked.

Mary glanced over again. "You mean, what do I think they do for a living?"

"Who do you think they are? What relationship do you think they are to one another?"

"Well, she could be his mother and they're simply meeting for lunch. Or they could be work colleagues. They could even be doing business." She shrugged her shoulders, indicating she didn't see his point.

"My guess is that they are on the brink of an affair. And this is their first date," Tony said, before depositing a piece of tomato into his mouth.

"But that's mere speculation." She laughed. "You've no proof of that."

He wiped his mouth with a napkin. "The woman is in her thirties. Her top is far too low, the skirt too short and black stockings? High heels? She looks like a tart. She'd be fired turning up at work like that. Then, the biggest giveaway, the raincoat."

"What? What about the raincoat?"

"It's September! Who wears a raincoat in California in September? It's lightweight and covers well. She obviously didn't want the neighbors seeing what she was wearing when she left the house. Then there's the guy. His body is half over the table. He can't believe his luck. Older attractive woman bored out of her mind, looking for a bit of fun. Lots of sex with no strings attached. It's what every young guy dreams of. And check out her body language. Her legs are crossed and her free leg is wafting up and down. And she's playing with her earring – she's game alright."

"So what if they are having an affair? What's your point?"

"My point is. What you see and what I see are two different things. It really doesn't matter if I'm right and you're wrong, or vice versa. You have a reality about them. And I have mine. They are both valid, up to the point where we would go over and ask. It's all just a matter of perception. Which beckons the next question. What is reality?"

Mary shook her head. "Now you've lost me."

"Just indulge me for a moment. Do you, like most people, think reality is what you see, feel and touch?"

"Well, I guess so," she said, frowning.

Tony pointed a firm finger at her. "Reality is only a concept. Reality is only a creation of the mind. And because one can't ensure that one will have another thought because for instance, they might have a heart attack and die or get killed in a car crash, the concept of a tangible reality is nonsensical."

"This is all very interesting. But I don't see what this has to do with my job or the fact that I can't get promoted?"

"Well, as I see it, you've got two options. You can continue playing a role that others have carved out for you. Or, you can change the perception, by consciously becoming the person you want them to think you are."

Mary's face brightened. *God, I'm good*, he thought. "You know, humans are pretty insignificant, when you think about it. It's not only naïve but damned egotistical to think that we are significant when you consider the infinite size of the universe. Don't take yourself so seriously, Mary. Look, the only thing you need to take care of, is the moment. Are you happy being who and where you are now. There's an infinite amount of choices out there. But people tend to limit themselves by how others perceive them. They give too much credence to why they can't do something rather than how to get what they want, because of other people's influences. If you can grasp that, then you can run rings 'round the fuckers, by consciously being who you need to be to get what you want. You'll be surprised how quickly things turn around. You may feel a bit of a fraud for a time, but once you start 'role playing' and getting results, it's worth the effort."

"But this is all very well and good, but it doesn't help me decide whether to stay in the police service. Do you think I should leave?"

"That's a decision only you can make," he said, pointing his knife at her.

It was obvious to him that Mary had little self-esteem. He felt sorry that she'd ended up this way. *Must be the father,* he reasoned.

"Look, Mary. It's a dog-eat-dog life out there. We have to fight for survival, just like any other animal on this planet. Everyday there's a battle, physically and emotionally going on between humans and the only way to survive is to learn the rules of combat. Both in the relationship game and in the career game."

"That's really cynical."

"Maybe. I'm just viewing it from a different window."

"OK then," she said, with a wry smile. "How do you play the career game?"

"What does it really take to make it in the police force? Why are your colleagues more successful than you? What do they do that you don't? All that you've told me so far, apart from intimidating their competition, is how corrupt they are. So do you think that has any bearing on them getting promoted?"

"Oh!" Mary, leaned back in her chair.

"Seems to me, you've been sitting on the sidelines. You've not been playing the 'police force game' at all. There are always unspoken, but significant formulas to success in the career world and the winners are those who are able to discover and capitalize on them. You've either got to jump in with both feet and play their game, or if you haven't got what it takes, quit! But," he pointed at her with his knife again "never, ever sit on the sidelines. That'll eat you up."

Mary's face brightened. "You're right, I've been giving this job 150% while others far less competent than me have shot through the ranks!" She fell quiet, pre-occupied, like she was replaying and re-evaluating some previous incident. She sighed and adjusted her seating "Boy, have I had my eyes opened. It all makes sense now. And you're absolutely right, this has been eating me up." She touched his hand. "Thank you, David. You've no idea how much you've helped me."

Tony smiled. He was really chuffed with himself. He loved this philosophical bullshit. Some he'd read, but most he made up as he went along.

They continued eating the rest of their lunch in silence. He could almost hear her thoughts processing his words, as she ate her pizza.

At the same time, Tony felt the walls closing in on him. He was both elated and disappointed by this newfound attraction. With other women, second dates always disappointed him. He could always see through the façade his date portrayed on their first encounter. It was expected, and he'd been OK with it, because the relationship did not advance beyond the bedroom. But Mary was different. He felt that she was the real deal; totally open, no pretense, what you saw was what you got. She didn't play games and contrary to being disappointed, he was even more besotted with her. And there lay his dilemma.

Typical, he thought, after months of planning, at the final hour, he'd found his soul-mate. Of course, he was under no illusion. The odds were heavily stacked against them. She was a cop and he a contract killer, albeit retired. But then, he couldn't just walk away, not now. It felt far too messy. He needed a clean cut conclusion.

"How's the pizza?" he asked.

"Really good," she said. "You want a slice?"

"Sure."

He watched her cut him a piece of pizza with her long seductive fingers and place it on his plate.

She didn't need to know about his past, he thought. This morning as he was scouting for Sylvia, he realized he could see himself doing this kind of work; low-key surveillance, interrogation, bodyguard etc on a consultancy basis. Then, quite legitimately, he could call himself 'private investigator'.

All he needed was a socially acceptable title. Personally, he didn't think there was any difference between what he did now and the role of a private investigator. As far as he was concerned, there was a moral line once crossed, made no difference whether you were a snoop or a killer. However, he was grateful that society didn't view it that way. But even so, Mary, with her seemingly high moral standards, might not approve of his plans. He needed to know fast. She caught him staring at her. She blushed and sipped some of her water.

Tony rubbed his chin, formulating a plan.

"I have something to admit," he said.

"Oh, and what's that?" she said smiling.

"I'm not just a bodyguard."

Her eyebrow rose. He couldn't work out whether she looked intrigued or suspicious. He'd have to go for it.

"I do a bit of private investigating in my spare time. It kinda blends nicely with my day job."

"Hmm. I can see that," Mary said pensively.

"Well, the thing is, I've got a job tonight. Why don't you come along?" Tony chewed his pizza, trying to gauge her reaction. She was quiet, seemingly weighing up the pros and cons.

"It's nothing illegal, is it? You know, I could get into a lot of trouble ..."

"Oh, no, it's nothing heavy," he quickly interjected. "It's just a domestic. I need to ask a guy a few questions, that's all. You know a lot of cops become private investigators."

She didn't answer.

"Come on. What harm can it do?" he prompted.

"Oh, why not," she finally said.

"Great. I'll call you tonight around 5:00 pm and tell you were to meet."

15

Sally walked along a street somewhere biblical. The men were dressed in striped kaftans and some wore fezzes. The women were completely shrouded in black, only their eyes were visible to the world. The street was lined with market traders and customers who bartered over fresh produce. It was so bright that everything seemed washed out and the sounds, muted. She felt as though she was part of an old, frayed, worn out movie, but even so, it felt real.

'Where's John,' she heard herself think, with more clarity than usual.

"You know the answer to that," replied an unfamiliar male voice. Although the voice wasn't hers, it came from inside her head. She was neither frightened nor upset by its message, it seemed logical. Somehow, she knew that this was how it was supposed to be and John was a name she would soon not be able to recall. After all, she was dead, wasn't she?

In front of her was a modern hotel. She walked toward it, but before she got to the door, she was in the foyer, reading through the employment section of a newspaper. Two young teenage girls in short, modern dresses laughed loudly as they joked with one another. They looked as though they'd spent a night on the town. She wished she were young and free enough to join them.

"What does she think she's doing?" said another voice. This time the voice came from behind.

"It's OK," replied the first voice, who was now also behind her, and no longer inside her head. "It's her way of dealing with it. She'll get there in the end."

She turned to see who was talking about her.

Sally woke up and heard a car drive away. Panting and sweaty, she scanned the room, confirming that she was alive. *Oh God, it seemed so real.*

A yellow post-it note covered the alarm clock and a steaming cup of coffee placed by its side, on top of a book. She sat up and plucked the note from the clock's face. The time read 7:58 am. The note was written by her mother. "Hired a car. Gone to the city to do some shopping. Meeting an old friend for lunch. Back around 3:00 pm. Love, Mom."

She stretched out her creased body, picked up the coffee and sipped it. Although she had every intention of running that morning, she was far too blue to rally herself. It wasn't just the dream. It was John. He hadn't returned home last night and his phone message hadn't sounded the least bit concerned that she hadn't picked up the receiver. *Bastard!*

She put down the coffee and picked up the book. It was *'Perfect Relationships*,' the one she'd been reading the night of the shooting. She opened it at the place where she'd left off.

"Relationships are what you let them become," wrote the author. "If you let your partner get away with unacceptable behavior, then the fault lies with you, as well as with your partner."

How can someone possibly make such a broad, off-the-wall statement like that! It's never that simple! Irritated, she threw the book on the floor.

Sally heard the side gate bang. She left the bed to investigate. Peering through the drapes, she could see Mike's truck, with its tailgate down, parked by the curbside. There were large plants on its bed. *What's he doing?*

She put on her bathrobe and went into the living room. Through the back window, she spotted some plants lined up by the fence, but no sign of Mike. Then there was knocking on the front door.

"Just a minute!" Deciding not to open the door to Mike in her nightclothes, she turned toward the bedroom, then stopped midway. *Oh, what the hell*, she thought, and went to answer the door dressed as she was.

"Oh, Detective Darnell!" He was the last person she expected and wanted to see. He was casually dressed in a brown leather jacket and beige trousers. His severely short-cropped hair and clothes reminded her of a combat pilot from a World War II movie.

"Mrs. Pringle. Good morning. I have a few more questions, but I see it's not a good time," he said, eyeing her nightclothes.

"John's not home," she said curtly, clasping the top of her robe.

"Actually, it was you I wanted to speak to."

Sally felt equally irritated and intimidated by him. What else could he possibly ask? She spotted Mrs. Horrendous Hernandez, as usual, peering from behind her drapes. She stepped back and held the door wider, so the detective could enter.

"Thank you," he said, stepping inside. She poked her head out of the door and looked without success for Mike. She waved across to Mrs. Hernandez. The drapes quivered as she disappeared from view. *That'll teach the nosey bitch!*

Sally closed the door. "Please sit down detective. If you'll excuse me a moment."

"Yes, of course."

She went into her bedroom. She grabbed some underwear from the top drawer of her dresser, a blue cotton dress from her closet and slipped off her nightclothes. She started dressing, wondering what the detective might ask her. She untied the belt on the dress and slipped it over her head. *This time, it's going to be a two-way street,* she thought. She retied the belt behind her back and frisked her hair, before giving herself a once over in the mirror.

Sally returned to the living room, strutting past the detective into the kitchen. "So detective, have you got any further with the investigation?"

"Well, yes and no." He got up and followed her.

She poured a couple of coffees from the percolator and handed one to him.

"Thank you," he said, taking it from her. "We've interviewed several students at the local high school, but so far we haven't come up with anything conclusive. We have eliminated a number of copycat incidents. But it's really slow going." Darnell sipped his coffee. "I see you've already fixed the fence?" he said, glancing over his shoulder.

"Yes, one of the builders fixed it yesterday. Oh, that was OK, wasn't it? You have finished with the backyard?"

"Oh, yes we're done collecting evidence here."

"Just how many legitimate incidents do you have?" she asked, attempting to keep control of the conversation.

"Nine, five from BB guns and four from the same rifle. Mrs. Pringle, have you and your husband lived in Fenton long?" the detective asked, suddenly changing tack.

"About four years," she replied evenly.

Over Darnell's shoulder, she spotted Mike through the window, carrying more plants. He crossed the garden and placed them besides the others.

"Really," he said. "You know, your husband doesn't strike me as the suburban type? Particularly, with him coming from New York."

How did he know that? He must have done some digging. Darnell must still suspect him. That's ridiculous! John's an insensitive pig, but he's no criminal.

Well, appearances can be deceiving!" she snapped. "Initially, John didn't want to move to Fenton, but I think he's settled here now."

Darnell sipped his coffee. She felt his eyes penetrate hers.

"What in particular did you want to ask me?" she said sharply.

"Have you noticed any strangers hanging around in the last couple of weeks? Someone who just seemed out of place?" He put down his coffee and pulled out his notepad from the inside pocket of his jacket.

"No. You asked me that yesterday!"

He flicked through his notepad then suddenly stopped. "Well, one of your neighbors, a Mrs. Hernandez, across the street at number 21, noticed a dark blue sedan parked outside her next door neighbor's house about ten days ago and then a second time, two days later. She said the man had a shaved head, a dark complexion, maybe foreign. She put him between 30 and 35 years of age. She thought he could have been surveying your house. Ring any bells?"

Trust Mrs. Hernandez to sidle into the investigation. A dark blue car? "No."

"Could it belong to someone working on your house?"

"No. The only men working here are the ones you've already seen and they all drive trucks."

"OK. Well let me know if you see the car or anyone bearing that description."

Sally nodded.

He snapped his notepad shut and returned it to his jacket pocket. "You know, this is the first time this town has had anything this serious. I know, I've reviewed the incident files. The only other crimes are pretty trivial by comparison. Domestic disputes, kids shoplifting and would you believe it, someone stole plants from Palmers Nursery yesterday. I'm thinking of moving here myself," he chuckled.

Sally smiled and sipped her coffee. She spotted Mike crossing the lawn with more plants. Mike's words ran through her head like an express train. "*Cheap, provided you aren't fussy where they came from.*" *Oh my God, he's stolen them.* She snorted coffee down her nose.

"Excuse me," she said, coughing.

Mike waved at her from the backyard. He seemed pretty pleased with himself, pointing over his shoulder towards the plants. He couldn't have known that Darnell was there, because the detective hadn't arrived in a patrol car. Thankfully, Darnell had his back to the window.

Sally glanced at her watch. "Oh, is that the time?" She took a few steps to the door. "Err, well detective, if I think of anything else, I'll be sure to let you know." Darnell followed her to the door. He seemed slightly affronted that she was rushing him out.

Mike tapped on the window. Both Darnell and Sally turned around. Mike's smile suddenly froze, leaving a silly, stilted grin on his face. The plant he was holding, gradually slid down the windowpane, then disappeared around his back. She cringed. The last thing she needed was to be accused of receiving stolen goods.

"I'll be there in a moment!" she shouted to Mike. "My gardener," she explained to the detective.

He just nodded. "I'll keep you informed of any further developments."

Mike had disappeared. Fearing he still had more plants left in his truck, she slipped in front of Darnell, momentarily blocking his exit, giving Mike some time to make his escape. "Oh, by the way. I went to a neighborhood meeting last night," she said, pressing a hand on the door. "Of course, there was a lot of talk about the shootings and I was asked to invite you along to the next meeting."

Mike's truck made pitiful coughs, as he tried to kick it into life. Scotty started barking.

"It's not really my department," he said. "You should contact the community services officer. But I would doubt if he would be willing to attend any public meeting focused specifically on the shootings."

Come on, come on, thought Sally. Above the dogs incessant yelping, she heard the belligerent rumble of Mike's truck, as it was forced to life. Then a loud grinding noise, as he put it into gear.

"However, I can ask him to give you a call."

Finally, she heard the truck pull away. "Oh, that would be great. Thank you." she said, opening the door.

"Well have a nice day, Mrs. Pringle." Darnell headed quickly down the drive. She closed the door. *How could Mike be so stupid!*

She left a scathing message for him on the contractor's answering machine. As she was halfway through it, the phone started beeping. Someone was trying to get through. She quickly pressed the button on the other line, half expecting a contrite John. Immediately, she heard screaming and held the receiver away from her ear.

"Hello, Sally it's Marie! Hold on a second would you? For God's sake Bobby, give it a rest!" Marie shouted over the din.

Sally then heard music. Immediately, the screaming subsided.

"TV is a Godsend," Marie sighed. "How are things?"

"Fine," she said, not feeling fine at all.

"I called and left a message yesterday. When you didn't call back I got a little worried. It's not like you," Marie said.

"You did? Oh, yes, I remember now. I was listening to a message when the power cut out. That must've been yours," Sally said.

"Well, never mind that now. I know it's short notice, but would you like to meet for lunch down at 'The Hole?' "

"Lunch? Today?" Usually, she would have jumped at the chance, but she was still wound up about John and Marie was a sleuth at reading people. She would know straight away that something was up.

"Oh, come on. It'll do you good. Besides, I need a break. The kids are driving me nuts. Meet me at one o'clock."

Sally detected an element of pleading in her voice. "OK, why not?"

Sylvia sat on a bench in Union Square waiting for Tony. She glanced around, then checked her watch again. He was twenty minutes late. She was just about to leave, when she spotted him at the edge of the park. He wore a black leather jacket, dark jeans and walked towards her with a brisk, confident swagger. He glanced casually around, as if making sure he was safe. Maybe he was concerned that she had called the cops, she thought. She loosened the scarf she'd used to conceal the bruising around her neck.

"Hi," he said, dropping beside her. He made no apology for being late. "I waited outside John's apartment building this morning. He left at approximately 8:00 am. A few minutes later I went up to search his condo. Glad I waited. When I got out of the elevator a dark-haired woman about 5'4", 120 lbs was leaving his apartment. She seemed pretty wired. She flew past me."

"The bastard!" Sylvia said.

He slipped his hand inside his jacket and produced a wallet. "Her name is Leslie Meadows, 32 years old. She's John secretary. Leases an apartment on Dwight. She's got about $20,000 in the bank, a few pieces of jewelry, very little family, just a mother."

She opened the wallet. Her eyes fell on the driver's license of an attractive, young brunette.

"How did you get this?"

"I lifted it," he said, matter-of-factly.

She shook her head. "Oh."

"She has credit cards jointly in her own and your son-in-law's names. There are men's clothes, about your son-in-laws' size, in her apartment. Here's her address, telephone number, their bank account and credit card numbers." He handed over a list of the details. "It's obvious that John's playing around, and from the look of it, for quite some time."

"How do you know all this?"

"From her apartment. Look keep up will ya! I'm short on time."

"Sorry…. Do you think he's trying to have Sally murdered?"

169

"Having an affair is hardly a prerequisite for murder. And there wasn't anything in John's or the tart's apartment to indicate that he is. But I think we should have a little talk with him, don't you?"

Sylvia nodded.

"What kind of car does he drive?" he asked.

"He's always driven BMWs, I think the last one he bought was black."

He suddenly jumped up from the bench and briskly walked away.

"Where are you going?" she shouted after him. "Tony!"

"Later!" he yelled.

She glanced at the wallet and then at Tony as he disappeared into the crowd. He's a fast worker. This guy's a professional. If anyone could get to the bottom of this, he could.

16

When Sally first moved to Fenton, she and Marie had often lunched together. Marie would whine about how dull and backward Fenton and its people were. She seemed to have had as much passion for leaving it, as Sally had in moving there. But after Marie's fourth child, the lunches suddenly stopped. Sally assumed she was too busy, though she made regular appearances at the Tuesday writing group.

Sally was the first to arrive at 'The Hole.' Although it was hot, she preferred sitting outside to the freezing, air-conditioned inside of the bar. She ordered a diet Coke and took the only table available, conveniently located by the sidewalk and shaded by a walnut tree.

Main Street was a height of activity. Cars were parked diagonally on both sides and since there was a twenty minute parking restriction, plenty of cars cruised up and down searching for an opportune space. She spotted Marie walking on the other side of the road, waiting for a gap in the traffic. Bobby was screaming and squirming in his stroller, trying desperately to escape. A brown Jeep Cherokee stopped mid-traffic to let them across.

In contrast to the other day, Marie was pretty well groomed. She wore a long, green and yellow flowered patterned dress and her hair was neatly tied away from her face. She waved a thank you to both the Cherokee and the white Honda sedan, which had stopped in the opposite direction to let her across.

"Hi," shouted Marie above Bobby's wail as she approached.

Sally moved the chair nearest the sidewalk out of the way, in order to make space for the stroller. Marie pushed it towards the table, set its brake and sat down on the chair next to it. Bobby made such a racket, that he attracted the attention of a young couple on the next table.

"Oh, here you are, have them!" Marie offered Bobby a set of keys. He snatched them from her, immediately fell quiet and started sucking on them. "I know I'll suffer from his upset stomach later, but I just need a moment's peace."

The waiter returned with Sally's Coke.

"Is that all you're having?" Marie asked. "Bring us two gins, a bottle of tonic water and a couple of menus," she said to the waiter.

Nodding, the waiter promptly disappeared inside.

"But it's lunchtime!" Sally said.

"I know, I know. But it's a long time since I've been out. And anyway, I need a stiff drink."

"Bobby's seems tired. Look, he's falling asleep, bless him."

Marie glared at him. "I should hope so, after all the din he made this morning. So, who was on television last night?" she said, suddenly changing the subject.

"No! I wasn't! How did I look?"

"Awful. All nose and teeth." Marie teased.

Sally's hand went to her mouth. "Please don't tell me I was in my dressing gown."

"No!" she replied, shaking her head. "I'm just kidding. You looked fine."

The waiter returned with their drinks, menus and two glasses of water. Marie snatched one of the gins and the bottle of tonic water from the waiter's tray before he had time to place them on the table. She poured a smidgen of tonic in the gin and swallowed the drink down in one gulp. "Bring another," she said, replacing the empty glass on the tray.

Sally was a little taken aback. *It must have been a very long time since she's been out!*

"So what did you think about Joan the other day?" Marie asked.

"Oh, poor Joan. She must be devastated!"

"Men. They're such bastards!" Marie snapped. "They come home from work and expect to be waited on hand and foot. What do they think we do all day, sit on our butts watching soap operas!" Her head swayed from side to side. She looked and sounded manic. "I mean, Joan had invested over 30 years in that marriage. And look what she got for it!"

"I know. It's really hard to believe. I … "

"And then, when they're done!" Marie ranted, her voice even louder. "When you're old and worn out. When your

173

body can't take anymore! They're off!" she said, wafting her hands about. She bent closer to Sally. "But you know, it's our own fault. We trust them too much. They're like little kids, pushing the boat out just a little at a time. All the time!"

The couple at the next table turned around and sniggered. The waiter returned with another gin. Again, Marie swallowed the drink as soon as it hit the table, this time, straight up. "Keep them coming," she said to the waiter.

Sally became anxious. She had never seen her so agitated. She'd seen her cross before but had never seen her go off like this. "Are you OK? Marie, has something happened?"

"Me? No, I'm fine. You know me, I'm always fine!" she snapped. For a moment Marie's face creased up. Then pulling herself together, she smiled weakly at her. "I've got enough kids to fill an orphanage. Why wouldn't I be alright?"

Dumbfounded, Sally wondered what was wrong with her. Marie leaned forward and momentarily covered her face with her hands. "No, I'm not all right. I'm pregnant again!" she said, tears suddenly cascading down her cheeks. The couple next to them suddenly left their table and headed inside.

Bewildered, Sally searched her purse for a tissue. "But that's wonderful! I don't understand," she said, handing her a tissue. "Why are you so upset?"

The waiter returned with another gin. Marie attempted to take the glass from the tray again, but this time Sally intercepted it. The waiter moved to the empty table and stacked up the dirty plates, eyeing Marie disapprovingly.

"Five of the things. I mean, can you imagine!" Marie reached for the gin.

Sally held it away from her. "You shouldn't be drinking."

"No, I should be taking a bath in it!" Marie yelled. Bobby suddenly woke up, dropped the keys on the floor and started crying again. Marie glared at him and started crying herself. "How am I going to cope?" she whimpered through the tissue. "I can hardly keep it together as it is."

Sally picked up the keys, wiped her napkin over them and gave them back to Bobby, who immediately fell silent.

"Oh Marie, I'm so sorry. How does Kent feel about it?"

"He doesn't know," she replied, blowing her nose. She glanced around to see if anyone was near enough to hear her, then bent closer to Sally. "Promise me, you won't say anything to anyone. Not yet," she whispered.

"Of course, I promise. But you can't keep it a secret for long," Sally replied.

"Do you know where there's one of those clinics?"

"What kind of clinic?" *She couldn't mean.* Marie!"

Marie shushed her, then bent forward again, "I'll kill myself before I have another child."

"But you're Catholic," Sally whispered. "You're against abortion. Aren't you?"

"Don't talk to me about that. I've had a belly full of Catholicism. You've no idea what it's like. If that husband of mine would agree to use condoms, I wouldn't be in this mess. He uses religion as an excuse. I should've taken the pill. He wouldn't have known. What a fool!"

"Are you ladies ready to order?" the waiter asked curtly.

175

"No, we're not!" Marie yelled, making Sally flinch. The waiter straightened, obviously affronted and strode away.

"This isn't like you. You don't know what you're saying." Marie was like the storybook mother. She always had kids in her house, if not her own, someone else's. Her house was like a kindergarten.

"Don't patronize me! How could you know what it's like to have kids?"

Sally gasped. Marie's words cut her to the core. Hurt and embarrassed, she faced the ground.

"I'm sorry. I didn't mean that," Marie said.

For a split second she felt compelled to leave. Of all people, Marie knew how much she'd wanted children. She glanced at her, Marie seemed truly mortified. "What a pair. I can't have any and you can't stop having them." Sally said.

"I know. God has a strange sense of humor." Marie blew into the tissue. "You know, after Bobby was born I was so depressed. I realized that I'd never have a life of my own. I've done nothing."

"That's not true. Having and raising children is not nothing. It's just about the most important job in the world."

Marie shook her head dismissively. "Funny how people say that - 'job'. They never say career, do they? Sally, raising kids is a nightmare. You get no thanks. No-one gives you credit and no-one thinks you're worth listening to; it's like you're invisible. You're tired all the time. And when the kids start screaming, it's torture. I feel old, worn out. This isn't a job, this is hard labor!"

Sally studied her face. She did seem tired and beaten. "I had no idea you felt like this. Why didn't you tell me?"

"Because … " she said, blowing her nose. She glanced away from Sally and reddened, then faced her straight on. "Well because I was jealous."

"Jealous of what? Jealous of me! What on earth for?"

"Because you have it all. You've been places, you had a career, and you've stood on your own two feet and then you married well. What have I ever done? I was pregnant three weeks after leaving high school." Marie shook her head. "It's different for you. You don't view marriage and kids like a life sentence. I've even convinced myself, that you would be a better mother because you want it so much. But me? It's sucking the life out of me. Everyone thinks I'm just so … so happy, so frigging content. I can't stand it."

So that's why she stopped meeting me for lunch.

"Of course, Kent doesn't know all this, he's so happy with it all. Good old reliable Marie he calls me, like some old frump. I wanted more. What's wrong with wanting more?" she asked, her eyes welling up again. She looked away, as though she suddenly felt guilty for asking such a question.

"We all want more," Sally finally said. "And usually they're the things we can't have." She grasped her friend's hand. "Promise me though, you'll think hard before you make a decision about the baby. At least give yourself a couple of days to think about it."

Marie smiled weakly through her tears and nodded. "I will, I promise. You're such a good friend. I'm so relieved to get this off my chest. It's been eating me up. And I'm really

177

sorry we stopped seeing each other like we used to. I can see now it was a big mistake." She drank some water.

"Let's promise not to let it happen again," Sally handed her another tissue. Since Marie had confided in her, she felt compelled to tell her friend about her own fears, that her own life wasn't as good as it appeared. "Marie, John and I…."

"Hey, isn't that Joan?" Marie said.

"Where?" She surveyed the street, and spotted Joan in front of Jackson's, the attorney's office. "Yes, it is." She was talking, or more precisely trying to dodge Doreen Anderson.

"Poor thing's been cornered by Doreen. I bet she's giving her hell," Marie said. "Joan! Over here!"

Joan scanned around, obviously hearing her name, but not knowing from where.

"Joan!" shouted Sally and Marie in unison.

Finally, she spotted them and hotfooted it over, with Doreen Anderson trailing her, like a dog on heat.

"Hi," Joan said, flustered.

"Hi, Joan, Doreen," Marie said.

"Hi," Doreen replied tersely, barely acknowledging her. Marie pulled a rude face at her.

"So, is it true? Has something happened between you and Eric?" Doreen asked.

Joan looked crimson with embarrassment and anger. She took a deep breath, then blurted. "Mind your own business, you nosey bitch!"

"Oh, wow," Marie exclaimed.

Doreen's mouth dropped open, seemingly lost for words. Then, she spun on her heel and sped away.

"You go girl!" Marie cheered, picking up the gin. Sally went to grab it from her but Marie was too quick.

"Here," Marie said, offering the drink to Joan, a renowned teetotal. "Take it. You've got nothing to lose. I can see the local headlines now, 'Respected local socialite falls from grace.' "

Joan took the gin and drank it straight down. She was smiling, but her eyes watered either from the gins strong aroma, or because she was upset. Sally suspected both.

17

Later that day, under the influence of too many gin and tonics, Sally found herself gardening in over 100^0F of blistering heat. Reasoning that the authorities were too preoccupied with the shootings to be concerned with her meager booty, she decided to plant Mike's bushes, along with the plants her mother had bought the previous day.

She tried breaking the ground with her shovel, but the baked adobe soil was as hard as nails. So she sprayed the ground with sharp streams of water from a hosepipe. The sun blazed overhead making her feel lightheaded. What a week, she thought. Record weather and record woe, something had to break. Although she would never wish any bad luck on her friends, it was comforting to know that she wasn't the only one with problems. All three women had commiserated with each other over their personal problems and all of them had far too much to drink. *I bet Joan's sleeping it off now.* She chuckled, remembering how only an hour ago they had staggered up Main Street to their respective homes.

A small pool of water had developed around Sally's rubber boots. As she turned off the hose, her thoughts returned to John. *What am I going to do?* She jumped onto the shoulder of the shovel, trying unsuccessfully to cut through the earth and stumbled into the puddle of water, splashing her legs. *We can't go on like this! I'll have to confront him.* She'd start by asking him why he hadn't returned home last night. Of course, he would say that he'd been tied up at work and try to make her feel foolish and guilty for asking. But this time, it wouldn't wash. She just wasn't going to live like this anymore.

"Hi," said a voice behind her. It was Andy.

"Hi," she replied.

He was wearing a black vest and washed out denim shorts. She blinked away the temptation to stare at his chest.

"Well, you'll be pleased to know we'll be out of here tomorrow. Mike's done the bathroom and I'll have finished the closets today."

She smiled but was not pleased by the news. Another shift, even the long awaited end to the remodel suddenly seemed too much to bear.

"You look busy," he said.

"Yes. My mother bought me these jasmines, and Mike brought some shrubs over this morning." She felt dizzy. "I thought I'd try and plant them but the grounds too hard."

"Here let me."

She stumbled a little, as he relieved her of the shovel's support. She felt small and feeble as he dug through the ground like a knife through butter.

"Ok," he said, nodding to the plants. Slowly, Sally dragged over one of the jasmines. Andy squatted and helped her pry the bush from its plastic container. She blushed as their fingers momentarily touched. He seemed not to notice, but she, feeling the need for distance, stood up. She swayed from the sudden change in elevation. *I need to lie down.* He placed the plant in the hole, scooped up some earth and tenderly tucked it around the plant's base. His hair was almost white in the bright sunlight. She felt an overwhelming urge to run her fingers through it.

"My mother liked jasmines," he said, patting down the earth around it. "It was her favorite plant."

"Oh really. It's mine too."

Andy stood up. He was so close that some of her hair stuck to his face. His blue eyes penetrated hers, fixing her to the spot. He brushed her hair away from his face, and gently stroked it back around hers. She felt light as though the world had dropped away beneath her. There was complete stillness, just the two of them suspended in the moment.

Heavy banging propelled her back to reality. Someone was knocking on her front door.

Andy scanned the ground, obviously feeling awkward. She turned and sauntered into the house, trying hard to keep her balance.

She opened the door.

"Hi, darling." Her mother walked briskly past her. "You really should get that doorbell fixed," she said, disappearing down the bedroom hallway." Do me a favor and get me a glass of water, would you?" she shouted.

182

After closing the door Sally went to the kitchen. She filled a glass from the faucet while looking through the window for Andy. He had gone.

"How was your day," her mother asked, returning from the bedroom. Sally handed her the glass of water.

"Thanks love."

"I met Marie for lunch and well, a few of us had lunch together." She filled another glass of water for herself.

"Well that's nice."

"And how's your friend?" Sally asked.

"Grace! She's doing great. Retired two years ago …"

Her mother rattled on about her friend. Barely listening, Sally wiped the countertop. She was thinking about Andy and how he'd made her feel. Then, she thought about John, how he didn't make her feel. *How's that possible? The alcohol.* She stroked her brow with the back of her hand. *I need to sleep this off. Everything will make sense when this wears off.*

"Sally. Are you alright?"

"I'm fine?" She tried unsuccessfully to smile. She turned away in an attempt to hide her face. But she knew her mother had spotted something. "No, Mom. I'm not alright. None of its right," she said, facing her squarely.

"Come on, let's sit down," said her mother. "But I think it'd be a good idea if you take your boots off first."

A trail of mud covered the kitchen and hallway floors. Sally had forgotten to take off her rubber boots when she'd walked in from the garden to answer the door. She stepped out of them and followed her mother to the couch.

"Do you want to talk about it?" her mother asked.

Sally nodded no. But then blurted, "Well nothing seems to have gone the way I planned!"

"Like what?"

"This house for one," Sally said. "And John. And well, you and me! We don't see each other. When we do, I'm on edge all the time waiting for an argument to start! It's just not what I wanted!"

"I know. I know. But we're not so different from other families. People have their own lives, their own experiences, and it moulds them. They become different. It's not surprising families don't get along."

"That's my point," Sally said.

"What's your point?"

"People live their own lives. What life have I got? I hardly ever see John. And when he is home, he's frustrated, even though I try my very best to make things comfortable for him. And we never get any time to spend together. For all I know, he could be having an affair!"

There was a pause, as if her mother were mulling something over. "Well, perhaps you're just trying too hard, darling."

"You mean it's my fault!"

"No, of course not."

"Then, what did you mean?" Sally asked.

Her mother sat back. "When I married your father, everyone seemed so surprised. He wasn't my intellectual equal, they said. You're from completely different backgrounds, they said. Nobody expected us to last. You see, everyone assumed I would marry someone of a similar station. But all the other men I had known were only interested in getting their hands on my money. I was just a commodity. Then I met your father," she smiled. "Everyone thought he was a waster." Her mother stared into space. "And looking back, they were right."

"Mom!"

"It's alright, I would never say anything about your father that I wouldn't have said to his face. I had all the money we ever needed. He didn't care about money or what it could buy. He would have been happy living in a shack. Do you remember those old pair of brown trousers he used to wear?"

Sally nodded and smiled.

"He wouldn't even buy himself anything. I had to shop for him. I bought him lots of clothes, but he always wore those brown trousers, until one day I took a pair of scissors to them. And you know, he never raised his voice to me – not once. The point is, we didn't have to try to make each other happy. We just loved each other the way we were."

"Sally, you know how I feel about John," she continued. "And I don't like seeing you upset like this, but I also don't want to cause trouble. You have to make your own decisions. I know that now. I just want us to stay friends. But if you ever, ever need my help or advice, I'm here, OK."

Sally took her hand. "Thanks mom."

There was a muffled ringing sound of a telephone. Her mother reached into her purse and plucked out her cell phone. "Hello?" she answered. Suddenly her face became grim.

"OK, I'm on my way." She hung up.

"What's up?" Sally asked.

185

"Grace. It's her husband. He's had a heart attack. Her daughter's on her way from Seattle, but she won't be able to get here until tonight. She's asked me to go over."

"Oh, yes, you must."

Her mother picked up her car keys. "But I don't like leaving you like this?"

"I'll be fine now mom, honestly."

18

John sat at his desk, with one hand supporting his chin, the other holding the telephone to his ear. "Oh, for Christ sakes!" he yelled, listening to Leslie's voice on the recording.

"...and I'll get back to you as soon as I can. Beep." She hadn't come into work so he knew she was still upset. He'd already called his apartment, so he'd assumed she must be at hers.

"Leslie, pick up the phone." She could be shopping, taking her anger out on his wallet, he thought. But then again, she might be listening. "Honey, I'm sorry about this morning. I know I said some things I shouldn't have. I'm just as frustrated as you. But we have to be patient. I promise, we'll be together soon. You know I love you. Call me, please." He replaced the telephone receiver in its cradle.

Feeling drained, he wiped his hands over his face, regretting not handling her better. But that morning, he'd been tired and she'd caught him off guard, resulting in an almighty row as he left his apartment. Of course it was about the same old thing. When was he going to leave Sally?

"Do we have to go over this again?" he'd said. "I've told you, I've already set the wheels in motion. You'll just have to be patient!"

"Patient! We've been doing this for almost two years now!"

"Can we please discuss this another time, Leslie. I've got to get to work!"

"Well, you've got until the end of the week. Either leave the bitch or we're through!" She snatched the radio from the kitchen counter and threw it at him as he closed the door.

Before Leslie, Sally had been his perfect partner. Attractive, low maintenance and most importantly, filthy rich. Sex wasn't an issue. He'd been able to fulfill any shortfall there, with the occasional fling. It had been a good life, but when the shit hit the fan with the GDB deal, it was Leslie, his secretary, who'd come to his rescue. She'd been privy to all his business misdemeanors and supported him through it all. Of course, he couldn't have told the high moral Sally about it. For one, it would have revealed his true nature, because it wasn't exactly an authorized deal and secondly, she might have been persuaded by that bitch of a mother-in-law to leave him penniless. Leslie was a whole different kettle of fish. He saw her as a female version of himself, a survivor, as hard as nails, and clever enough to spot an opportunity when it appeared. He never thought he needed anyone, not until her. She had it all; cunning, looks, great sex, everything but money.

To relieve his hangover, John swallowed a couple of aspirins. The night before had been pretty awesome, he thought, smiling to himself. Leslie had what he called PMT,

188

pre-mounting tension, all day. She'd kept stroking and teasing him in the office. It was hard to concentrate when she was like that. She played the stranger in the elevator scene like some x-rated, low budget movie. They'd screwed as soon as he'd opened the door to his apartment. He'd thrown her against the wall. She'd bitten into his neck. "What about Sally," she'd teased.

"There's no Sally. Just you."

Her legs clung around his back.

"Sally's always here," she said, scratching his neck with her nails, making him even more excited.

"No babe, there's no Sally. Sally's gone."

She'd licked the side of his face. He'd turned his head, so she could slip her tongue down his ear. She knew that drove him crazy. He was in a different dimension when they were like that. Nothing else mattered. God, it made him horny just thinking about it.

19

John walked toward the elevator on the fourteenth floor, where Jennifer Musgrove from marketing stood. She smiled at him then blew out an impressive large, lime-green ball of gum. She belonged to the group of young women who refused to grow out of their teenage years. She must be at least 21 but wore a short, black leather skirt, and a low, pink skintight top. Far too cheesy for John's taste. The elevator dinged its arrival and the doors sprang open. Nice ass though, he thought, following it into the elevator.

"Hold it!" said a voice. Jenny pressed and held down the door open button, while shithead Luke Rainey stepped inside. "Thanks," he said, beaming her a wide lecherous grin. As expected, he didn't acknowledge John. She let go of the button and pressed the parking lot button. The elevator doors closed, and they promptly began descending.

Luke was vice president of the Corporate Debt Department at Smithfield Price. He was a sharp guy, who had inherited his position way before his time. Eighteen months ago, Luke's managing director was killed when he plowed his Porsche turbo into a wall on his way home from a closing party. Spotting an opportunity to empire build, John lobbied hard for him to become Glen's permanent replacement. In exchange, there had been a gentlemen's agreement. Luke would support John, if and when the occasion presented itself. They were working together on the GDB deal, a substantial leveraged rollup in the healthcare sector. With disastrous consequences, the financing fell off the rails before the deal was fully completed, leaving Smithfield Price and its most prominent clients holding worthless paper. When the shit hit the fan, Luke, the scumbag, said that he'd opposed the deal all along, but because he was still 'wet behind the ears,' felt that perhaps he'd missed something, so hadn't said a word. Without support, John was left to take the heat. Although he would probably have done the same if the shoe was on the other foot, it still stung.

"So how about you and me getting together this weekend," Luke asked Jenny.

"I'm busy," she replied. "I'm always busy." She gave him a distasteful scan and stepped away.

No chance there you little shit! John smiled.

"Perhaps ..." Luke whispered something in her ear.

"In your dreams," snapped Jenny, moving further away from him.

John chuckled. Luke turned and gave him a 'what do you think you're looking at!' glare. John returned the gesture with another chuckle. As soon as the elevator stopped and the doors opened, both Jenny and Luke veered right. He walked straight ahead.

"Goodnight!" He shouted to both of them.

"Goodnight," Jenny said. Luke, of course, didn't reply.

John rummaged through his trouser pocket for his car keys, while walking in the general direction of his car. He activated the vehicle's remote. The headlights flashed, revealing the car's location. He heard a car start up, then another. He turned and waved to Jenny, as she drove by. John opened his car door and slid into the driver's seat. Immediately, he felt something hard against the back of his head.

"What the!" He tried to turn around.

"Not so fast, buddy," said a male voice. "Keep facing forward."

God! It's a gun! John spotted Luke driving up the exit ramp. "What do you want?"

"We're going for a little drive, sonny. There's someone really anxious to talk to ya."

John glanced in his rearview mirror.

Catching his eye, the man said. "Oh, I'm sorry. I forgot to introduce myself. My name's Mad Bastard. And I'm particularly out of sorts right now. Because today, instead of sitting on some hot, sunny beach, with some equally hot woman, sipping cold beer, I'm here with you. So, I would really like to get this fucking job done as quickly as possible, one way … or another." He tapped the barrel of the gun on the side of John's head. "Get my drift?"

"Yes," He stammered.

"OK buddy. Let's go."

John slammed the driver's door shut and placed his briefcase on the front passenger seat. His hand quivered as he put his key into the ignition and started the car. Turning his head to reverse, he inadvertently stared down the barrel of the gun. He swallowed hard, glancing up at his abductor. The guy, he calculated, was in his mid-thirties. He had a darkish complexion, a shaved head and dark brown eyes.

"I said, let's go," the man hollered.

John reversed out of the parking space and for a split second thought about smashing into the car parked behind him. But there was no-one around, and he couldn't guarantee that security would pick it up right away on their monitors. And more importantly, he was in no hurry to find out how his kidnapper came by such a descriptive name.

After shifting into drive, the elevator sprang open and about half a dozen people spilled from it. Just as he was about to stomp on the accelerator, Mad Bastard shoved the barrel of the gun into the back of his neck. "Slowly does it," he said.

John slowly pulled away toward the exit. "Where are we heading?"

"Turn left out of the parking lot. You're on a need-to-know, so all you need to know is left or right! Right?"

"Right!" he replied.

"And all you need to answer is yes, right?"

"Right, I mean, yes," John said, exiting the parking lot. His hands were already sweaty from firmly gripping the steering wheel.

They were heading south on Montgomery. Traffic was light, since rush hour had lost its momentum. He drove at a slow, constant speed, hampered only by the occasional pedestrian, running across the street in front of him.

"OK, turn right at the next junction."

He thought his abductor sounded either Australian or English. *What was this about? And who the hell wanted to talk to me?* As instructed, he turned right at the next intersection. The traffic lights ahead were green. As they slowly approached them, John noticed a man on the sidewalk trying to hail a cab. He would have given anything to change places with him. He realized he needed to take action before they left the city, knowing that he'd have no chance to escape once they'd hit the freeway. He drove the car as slowly as he dared, praying that the traffic lights ahead would turn red. As dangerous as it was, he would have to take his chances and jump out of the car. However, the lights stayed green and he was forced to drive on. *Damn it!*

"Now move into the left-hand lane. You're going to make a left."

John did as he was ordered. At the crosswalk, a couple of people crossed in front of him, blocking his path. *This is it. I have to do it now.* Then, he heard a click and felt the barrel of the gun in his side.

"Don't even think about it, pal. From this angle, I can easily shatter ya kidneys, spleen and maybe even splatter the pasta you had for lunch all over the inside of ya posh car."

He knows what I had for lunch! Slowly, John pulled forward. As the path in front of him cleared, he turned left.

"Now, move over to the right lane and turn right at the lights."

He turned onto First and followed the line of traffic. They were heading for the Bay Bridge. They neared another set of traffic lights, which also stayed green. *Fucking typical!* He

194

drove onto the bridge unhindered and merged into the traffic. *Why's this happening? This isn't a random kidnap. He's obviously been tracking me. If it's money he's after, well he's picked the wrong fucking guy! But of course, Sally! Maybe he knows about her rich mother and thinks Sally's a softer touch and more likely to pay a ransom.*

John wiped the sweat from his eyes.

"Hey. Both hands on the steering wheel!" Mad Bastard said.

He quickly returned his hand. *Maybe, someone just wants to scare me. Well, they're doing a fucking good job!* He glanced at his kidnapper in the rearview mirror. The man seemed agitated. He was wiping his eyes with a handkerchief. *Is he crying?*

"Jesus. What's that smell?" Mad Bastard suddenly exclaimed. "Smells like a fucking boudoir in here."

At first, John had no idea what he was referring to. Then the scent hit his nose. 'Poison,' it was Leslie's favorite perfume.

"Christ!" Mad Bastard said. John glanced in the mirror again. He couldn't see him, but he heard the rustle of a plastic bag. The man straightened and held up the bag, which was dripping wet. *He must have trodden on it and smashed the perfume bottle inside.*

"Geez!" Mad Bastard opened his window and threw the bag out, making the Jeep behind swerve. Then he stuck out his head. This was John's chance. He sharply turned the steering wheel to his left, smashing his car into the Nissan in the next lane, throwing himself, Mad Bastard and his briefcase violently to the left side of the car. The gun fired. Tires screeched. Car horns blew. John tried to straighten

195

out. The Nissan veered off, narrowly missing a truck on its other side. Finally, John regained control of the car. He felt sure that he'd been shot, that he would soon feel the pain.

"You fucking idiot!" Mad Bastard shrieked. He jumped up and down in the back seat, like someone possessed. He pushed the gun into John's cheek. John held his breath and fought hard to keep his eyes open.

"Try anything like that again and you're fucked! Do ya understand!" spat Mad Bastard.

Traumatized, John couldn't answer.

"Do you! Understand!" Mad Bastard shrieked, stabbing John's cheek with the barrel.

"Yes I understand!" he screamed. "I'm sorry alright! Just don't shoot! Christ, I don't want to die. Please!"

Mad Bastard pulled the gun away. "Well, ya going the wrong fucking way about it! Fuck me! Man … look what you made me do?"

John had no idea what Mad Bastard had done. He was just relieved the bullet hadn't hit him but hoped that Mad Bastard, at the very least, had shot himself somewhere.

"Man, your car. Sorry, mate. I shot your car."

Does he really think I care about my car? He's nuts!

"I hate the fucking Germans, but they make bloody good cars. OK, now move over to the right lane."

He moved into the 880, San Jose and West Grand Avenue lane, disturbed by the way Mad Bastard had jumped from total rage to a sincere appreciation of mechanical excellence.

"OK, take the next exit and make a right at the stop sign.

John had once read that professional kidnappers made it difficult for their captives to later recall a route by keeping instructions simple and to a minimum. All his instructions were either to turn left or right with no mention of street names. He therefore concluded that Mad Bastard was a professional and had done this kind of thing before.

"Take the next right."

He approached the next set of lights and turned right onto Baaton, into an abandoned military base. John was familiar with the area. The year before he'd been approached by a shady property developer to finance the building of an exclusive sailing club and marina. He was a little surprised that Mad Bastard had picked somewhere relatively easy to locate.

He drove another hundred yards or so, then he was ordered to turn into a small parking lot in front of a large corrugated building.

"Pull up against that Tacoma."

John parked and turned off the ignition.

"I'll have them," Mad Bastard said, referring to John's car keys.

"OK let's go."

They climbed out of the car. John examined his kidnapper. He was short, but much wider and fitter than he was. John knew that he wouldn't stand a chance against him. He stared into his kidnappers eyes and was suddenly overcome by a disturbing thought. The guy hadn't bothered to disguise his face.

20

Alarmed by the fact that he might not get out of this alive, John stared into what he now regarded, his executioner's face. And Mad Bastard, as if reading his mind, grinned then shoved him towards the corrugated building. Slowly, John walked to the door, glancing furtively around, hoping that someone would spot them and alert the authorities. In the distance, he could hear the sounds of heavy machinery, but the immediate vicinity seemed deserted. The other outbuildings were disused military barracks and at the water's edge, an old rusty crane. It was obvious from the weeds in the concrete and garbage blowing around, that the area hadn't seen life for quite some time.

"Move it," Mad Bastard said, pushing him again.

The corrugated door moaned, as John opened it and stepped inside the building's cavernous interior. It was dim, illuminated only by natural shafts of daylight, bursting through some missing roof panels. He had no idea what the building had been used for, but its size, together with the huge doors at the far end, seemed big enough to house large aircraft. The metal roof panels crackled and chinked as the wind passed beneath them. Puddles of stagnant water lay on the concrete floor and a solitary metal chair was placed a few feet away. Mad Bastard let go of the door. It echoed pitifully behind them.

"David! I know him," said a female voice from the right. An attractive blonde about 5'6", dressed in jeans and a brown quilted jacket, walked towards them. If she knew him, then he probably knew her, John reasoned. She seemed vaguely familiar, but he couldn't place her. David, alias Mad Bastard pushed him towards the chair. He sat down gripping both sides of the seat and studied the couple. They seemed to be quibbling about something. The woman was visibly upset and David, seemed to be trying to pacify her. *Who the hell was she?*

Another gush of wind blew through the roof. John felt cold and clammy. Whoever they are, maybe he could strike a deal with them "Look, how much do you guys want?"

The couple immediately stopped talking and turned to face him. "My wife has money. I know she'll pay," he pleaded.

David whispered something into the blonde's ear. She walked over to a stack of chairs to John's right. She picked out a chair and sat down. David followed suit, picking up two chairs. He dropped one about ten feet in front of John and another chair to its side, making him flinch. The sound of metal against concrete echoed menacingly around the inside of the building. David lifted his foot onto one of the seats, and laid his gun across his bent knee. He pulled out a handkerchief from his black leather jacket and began polishing his weapon. There was a foreboding silence. The only sounds were the wind battling against the roof and the ominous, soothing resonance of cloth against metal. John eyed the empty chair with terrifying apprehension. He became aware that he was panting. He wiped his sweaty palms down his trousers. He glanced between his two kidnappers, wondering what this was about and how it would play out. He detected a hint of apprehension as his eyes momentarily locked with the blonde's, but then she turned away from him. David suddenly stopped polishing his gun and aimed it at John. He gasped and braced himself, staring into David's eyes. There was nothing decipherable in them, no coldness, no bitterness, no sympathy, just a bottomless pit of nothingness. David winked, breaking John's trance. With a satisfied grin, David spat on the gun and continued polishing it.

A car pulled up outside. He heard the vehicle's door slam and light footsteps crunch against the gravel.

This is it. John's heart knocked against his ribcage. A single line of sweat crept down his forehead and dripped into one eye. He briskly wiped it away. The metal door opened noisily. In walked a gray-haired, middle aged woman, wearing jeans and a red sweatshirt. *Sylvia? It looks like Sylvia, but her hair? What's happened to her hair?*

"Sylvia! Thank God!" John said, jumping from his chair.

"Hey!" David said, pointing the gun at him. John sat down again.

"How much do they want?" John asked.

Without breaking pace, Sylvia strutted directly to him, clenched her fist and smashed it across his face. "You no-good piece of shit!"

John cupped his hands over his smarting nose. "What the?" he said bewildered, peering up from a cowering position. Blood seeped through his fingers. "Fuck!"

"How dare you try to have Sally murdered!" she barked. He watched her pace in front of him like a caged tiger.

"What the fuck are you talking about?" John moved his hands from his face. Blood dripped to the floor. "Murder Sally? Are you nuts!"

David turned his chair around and sat leaning his arms on the back, facing him.

"For Christ's sake John, you could have filed for divorce," Sylvia yelled. "Half of Sally's money would have set you up for life. But no, you little shit! You wanted it all, didn't you! Well, you're not getting your hands on a penny now. Not a single, fucking penny. I'll see you in hell first!" She shook her hand. He didn't know whether she was preparing to hit him again or simply shaking pain from her hand.

"Have you completely lost your mind?" he said.

David got up and came toward him. Anticipating more punishment, John closed his eyes and held up his arm in defense. When nothing happened, he opened an eye. A handkerchief hung in front of his face. John took it from him and held it over his nose. David returned to his seat.

"Ouch!" John winced. His nose stung like hell. Then he smelled the perfume. It was the handkerchief that David had used to wipe the perfume off his clothes. David grinned at him.

Sadistic Bastard!

"I've been doing a little digging!" Sylvia continued ranting. "I know about your fuckup at the bank and about your affair."

"OK, yes. But kill Sally? That's crazy!"

"David, this is wrong," said the blonde. Everyone turned to her. She headed for the door. David left his chair, placed his gun in the back of his waistband and blocked her path. "I want no part of this," she said, trying to maneuver around him.

David grabbed her arm. "Trust me. Just five more minutes."

"Who is this?" Sylvia asked.

"Don't go, not yet," David said to the blonde. She glanced down at his hand on her arm then looked him squarely in the face. "Look David, I don't know who you are and frankly, I don't care. If this is what you call a little domestic, then I'm outta here. I'm not about to throw my career away for a common criminal."

"You're not. I can't explain right now. Just…just bear with me a little longer. Please, Mary?" he said.

"Tony, who is she? And why does she keep calling you David?" Sylvia asked.

John wanted to know the same thing. *Who are these people?*

Mary looked at Tony, alias, David, Mad Bastard, shook his hand from her arm and tried again for the door. But he stopped her again, this time by holding her shoulders.

"My name is Tony," he said. She tried to avoid his eyes. John racked his brains, trying to remember who she was. Then it came to him. *She's one of the cops on Darnell's team!*

202

"I know who you are!" he said. *Oh shit, maybe she's working undercover or something. Maybe there are more cops outside. You stupid bastard, you've probably blown it now!*

"Well?" Sylvia asked, "Can someone please enlighten me?"

"A cop," Tony replied. Finally, Mary looked at him. "She's a cop," he repeated.

"Oh, terrific," Sylvia said, throwing her arms up in the air. "That's just great!"

"You've set me up!" Mary said. There were tears in her eyes. "All that rubbish about, about reality. What's the reality now! You're a, whatever you are! And I'm a …. was a cop! Why did you do this to me? Do you get a kick out of screwing around with people lives?"

"I know how it looks," Tony said. "But trust me. Just stay a little longer. It's going to turn out fine, I promise."

"Get me out of here, for God's sake," John pleaded, desperately holding onto the fact that she may actually be armed. Mary glowered at him. At that very moment, he didn't think she looked particularly sympathetic to his cause.

"Oh, shut up, John!" Sylvia said.

"The truth is this guy hired me to kill his wife." Tony told Mary.

"I most certainly did not!" John spluttered. "You're crazy, the lot of you!"

"Mary, I messed up," Tony continued. "And I'm just trying to set things right."

He took hold of the back of her neck with one hand and touched her face with the other, forcing her to look into his eyes. "I know you probably don't believe this right now. But

203

you've done something to me. I can't explain it. And I know you feel the same. Don't you?"

Mary didn't move. John couldn't tell whether she was smitten or scared, but he could see she was pretty pumped. She was breathing heavily, her eyes were wide and watery, her face red. She glanced at Sylvia then at John. *Go Mary, go get help!* John thought, conjuring up his most earnest expression.

"Five minutes, that's all I'm asking," Tony pleaded. "Mary, please."

No, don't listen to him. Head for the door, thought John. But she didn't move. He knew that the longer she took to answer, the more likely she was to cave in to him. He saw Mary's face soften a little, his last hope evaporating before his eyes.

"Look guys," John said, trying another tack. "Besides being one hundred percent wrong about me, you're obviously screwing up what appears to be a perfectly good relationship."

Suddenly, Mary pushed Tony's arms off her, grabbed the gun from the back of his waistband, and aimed it squarely at John. "Shut up!" she shouted. John stiffened and stared at the shaking barrel.

"Sylvia? For God's sake!" he pleaded, holding up his hands in defense.

Tony stepped towards Mary. "Mary, it's alright. I know you're really upset. Give me the gun." Suddenly she turned the gun on Tony.

"Shut up, while I think," she said.

Tony didn't waver, he seemed as cool as ever. "Come on Mary, you're in no state to be holding that gun. Give it to me." He held out his hand.

"Shoot," John yelled.

Mary spun around and aimed the gun back at John. He cringed, expecting her to fire.

Tony went up to Mary's side. "I'm sorry for lying and for getting you into this. But shooting someone isn't going to get you out of it, is it? Five minutes, Mary, five more, short minutes and this will be over." She glanced up at him. "Now give me the gun," he said. Her arm shook even more erratically, as she turned her attention back to John again. "Mary, come on," Tony said softly. He moved closer to her ear and whispered something to her then slowly moved his hand down her outstretched arm until he reached her hand. Finally he took the gun from her. Breathing a sigh of relief, John slumped in his chair. He covered his face with his hands, praying for divine intervention. When he looked up again, Mary had returned to her seat and Tony squatted down in front of her. He seemed to be pacifying her. She looked dazed and of no use to John.

"Let's get back to business," Tony said, returning to his chair. "Who did you speak to in Chinatown?"

"I didn't speak to anyone in Chinatown," John said, wearily. "I haven't been there in years. I don't even remember where it is."

"He can't help himself," Sylvia said. "Playing for high stakes, hey, John! Either die or you win it all, is that the plan?"

He shook his head. "I don't know what any of you are talking about. I swear."

"Perhaps," Tony said, aiming the gun between John's legs, "he doesn't think we're serious."

John pressed his legs together. *Holy shit!*

"Once, I was in this, sort of legitimate government militia," Tony explained. He flicked the gun away from John's body. "You know, the kind that governments always deny exist but on occasion turn to for help." He flipped the gun around, like it was some plastic toy, "and I've seen some pretty horrific interrogation techniques in my time. We all had our preferred persuasive techniques. Slasher! now, what do you think was his favorite weapon."

It wasn't rocket science. "Knives?" John answered softly.

Tony nodded. "We worked together in Belize in '93. We'd just come back from reconnaissance. He was all excited, said he had a new record. We all knew what he'd meant, 'cause he was covered in blood. Two hundred and ten cuts he gave the poor bastard before he expired. Poor Slasher, went round the bloody bend in the end. He made the local barman play Russian roulette with him. He lost. I think it was his way of doing himself in."

John swallowed hard.

"Knives," Tony said, shaking his head dismissively. "Far too messy for me. No, this is my little persuader. Same principle though." He aimed the gun at John's head. John braced himself. "My record, fifty-two bullets. Fifty-two little nicks, here," he said, pointing John's shoulder, "and there," moving back to John's groin.

John cowered. *I'm going to die.* He started whimpering.

"And you know the best thing about it. You'll look perfectly fine at the funeral," he added. "That's a promise." He shot beneath John's chair. The sound of the blast reverberated around the building several times.

"No, no, no!" John cried. "Don't shoot! I don't want to die! For Christ's sake, Sylvia! I didn't do anything, I swear!" There wasn't a trace of sympathy on her face.

Mary was on her feet, her mouth open, concerned.

Please, John mouthed at her.

"Are you ready to talk?" Tony asked.

Realizing they weren't interested in the truth and that they'd already made up their minds he was behind the shooting, he succumbed. "OK," he said, wiping his eyes on his sleeve. "I did it," he sobbed.

"I knew it," Sylvia said triumphantly.

"Who'd you talk to in Chinatown?" Tony asked.

"Does it matter? I did it! Alright?" John said shaking, glancing between Sylvia and Tony. "You don't have to kill me. You want me to disappear right? Untie me, and I'm gone. Then everyone gets what they want. Right?" he cried.

Tony glanced at Sylvia, then got up and went over to her. "He didn't do it," he said softly.

"What?" Sylvia said.

"Oh … thank you … God!" John said, turning his face to the ceiling.

"He thinks you just want to get rid of him," Tony said. "He'll say whatever you want. But he's not behind the hit."

"So who is?" she asked.

Tony merely shrugged his shoulders. Still holding his gun, he went over to John, grabbed him by the shoulder and pulled him from his seat.

"Ok, we're done. Let's go," Tony said to Mary.

"Where are you taking me?" John asked, as he was dragged across the floor like a rag doll. *Surely, he's going to let me go.*

Sylvia rushed over to them. "Now, hold on! Not so fast!" She blocked their way. "You gave me your word, remember? You said you'd help me get to the bottom of this! And if he isn't behind the hit, someone else is. And they might try again!"

"Sorry lady, but I'm done." He moved around her, dragging John along with him.

"Help me, Sylvia!" John cried.

"Will you shut the fuck up!" Tony yelled. "I'm not going to kill you. You're not worth wasting a bullet. You pathetic piece of shit!"

So relieved, John almost thanked him. But then thought better of it. Even gratitude might send the lunatic into a tailspin.

"Mary," Tony said again. She started to follow them, then stopped in front of Sylvia. "Are you OK?"

"I'm dying of cancer and someone is trying to have my daughter murdered," Sylvia said. "Do you honestly think I'm OK?"

John and Tony were almost at the door.

"Wait," Mary said, suddenly hurrying towards them. Addressing John, she said, "Look, I don't know what kind of relationship you have with your wife. But even if she means nothing to you, surely you don't think she deserves to die?"

John didn't answer. He just wanted to leave.

"Where's this going?" Tony asked.

"Well, you and Sylvia just assumed that he hired the hit. You haven't even considered anyone else. I don't think it would hurt to spend a few more minutes going over the facts to see if we can come up with something."

"Mary. It's over. Let's get the hell out of here," Tony said.

"But I just feel so sorry for her," Mary nodded in Sylvia's direction. "And, well I think you owe it to her. Or, are you in the habit of going back on your word?" she asked sternly.

Tony cocked his head from side to side looking slightly coy.

I don't believe this, thought John.

"You wouldn't want Sally's death on your conscience. Would you?" she said, turning to John.

Go to hell, he thought.

"Especially when you're the prime suspect," she added.

"Darnell really suspects me?"

"Well yes. The spouse is always the prime suspect. And if the police don't make an arrest, you will always be under suspicion. Especially, when they find out you're having an affair."

John considered his options. *Even if Mary disappeared into the night with Tony, Sylvia wouldn't think twice about telling the police about me and Leslie.* He realized he would always be under scrutiny and not only by the Police. He might never get another decent job. "But what can I do?"

Tony let go of him.

Mary put her hands on her hips. "Well. We could start by making a list of possible suspects."

"But I don't socialize with murderers!" John said, affronted.

"I'm not suggesting that you do," she said. "All I'm saying is, someone holds a grudge against Sally or you, enough of a grudge to go to the trouble and expense of hiring a hit man. For all we know, you could be next!"

"Huh!," Tony scoffed.

John hadn't thought about that. She had a point. And he really didn't have a choice. Everything she said was right and well, Tony still had the gun. "OK, OK. But I think it's a waste of time."

Sylvia heaved a sigh of relief. He felt some satisfaction that she needed his co-operation, even though he knew, he'd had little choice in the matter. He sat down on one of the chairs and touched his nose wondering whether it was broken. He didn't know when, but it had stopped bleeding. He'd been too concerned about the fate of the rest of his body, to worry about it. All of a sudden, he felt a presence behind him. He turned. It was Tony. Realizing that he was sitting in his chair, John shot out of it. "Sorry," he said.

"I think this belongs to you." Mary threw something to Tony. He caught it and opened his hand. It was an inhaler. "Yes. But what are you going to do about it?" Tony asked.

"Later," she said, pointing a firm finger at him. John saw Tony suppress a grin – *smug bastard*.

Rearranging the seats. Sylvia approached John with another chair. She dropped it in front of him, one of its legs smashing down on his toe. It hurt, but he didn't let her see;

smiling at her through clenched teeth. She turned away from him, her back rigid with contempt. She dragged another chair towards the circle they had formed and sat down.

"OK," Tony told Mary. "It's your floor."

"Let's start with the obvious question," Mary said. "Is there anyone you can think of who would want to kill you or your wife?"

Oh god, this is going to take all night. "No," John said, folding his arms across his chest.

"Well what about the GDB deal?" Sylvia piped up. "Anyone get their fingers burnt badly?"

"No. Not really," he explained. "Most of the clients were filthy rich. It hurt the bank, but it hardy registered with them. They probably benefited from tax write-offs."

"What about your personal life?" Mary asked.

"Well, what about it?" John replied stiffening, glancing at Sylvia.

"Tell us about it?" Mary said.

"No!"

"Oh, don't mind me," Sylvia said. "I hired a detective years ago. I know you like a fling here and there. And that's the real reason you keep the apartment in the City."

She knew all along? Why hadn't she told Sally?

As if reading his mind she said. "I didn't tell Sally because frankly, she's so besotted with you, she wouldn't have believed me if I had. So go ahead, tell them!"

"What do you want to know?" John asked.

"Leslie Meadows?" Tony said.

"Hey, you're barking up the wrong tree there," he said. "She's pushy, and determined, but not stupid enough to try anything like this."

"Well she'd have good reason." Sylvia got to her feet and paced the floor. "You've been living together for well over a year. You've got a joint bank account together, credit cards. Maybe she got impatient. Maybe she thought, that if you weren't man enough to leave your wife, she'd take matters into her own hands."

She knows everything. "You bitch!" John snarled.

"Hey, don't talk to your mother-in-law like that!" Tony said, aiming the gun at him. "Have more fucking respect. Say you're fucking sorry!"

"I'm f…sorry! But Leslie wouldn't hurt a fly," John continued. "I mean literally, she's a, well she practices Buddhism."

"That's right," Tony said. "All sorts of weird shit in her apartment."

"You were in her apartment!" John yelled.

"Yeah. Yeah," Tony said nonchalantly, like it was no big deal.

Jesus, thought John.

What about other women?" Tony asked.

"There are no other women," John replied. "I'm loyal to Leslie."

"Oh you bastard!" Sylvia yelled.

"Yes, probably lots of those around too!" he retorted. "Look, I'm not in the habit of shacking up with murderers. I do have standards."

"Give me the gun!" Sylvia said, heading toward Tony. "I've just about had enough of him!"

Tony stood up and lifted the gun above his head, out of Sylvia' reach. "Now hold on a minute, you don't think this tosser is worth spending the rest of your life in prison for, do you?"

Sylvia didn't answer him straight away. John had overhead her telling Mary that she was dying of cancer. He panicked.

"Well yes, actually I do! Give me the gun! I'll kill the bastard!"

"Come on Sylvia," Mary said, standing behind her. "This isn't helping anyone. He's the only link we have to finding out what's going on here. Now, let's all sit down! And calm down!" she ordered.

Sylvia held up her hands in resignation. "You're right," she said, backing away. She glared at John. If looks could kill he wouldn't be breathing, he thought. She sat down. John was struck by how worn out she looked.

"And that means everyone!" Mary said to Tony. "Put the gun away Tony!" she ordered.

"OK, OK." He slipped the gun inside his jacket and they all sat down again.

"Let's look at it from another angle," Mary said. "Tony, how did the hit operate?"

"I have a friend I owe one to. He operated as agent."

"Then why don't you ask him?" John said glibly.

"It's not as simple as that," he replied, sarcastically. "There are several people involved in a hit. The longer the chain, the more people involved and the harder it is to trace the source to me and vice versa."

"How were you to be paid?" Sylvia asked. "What's your agent's name?"

"It gets dropped at a place and time of my choosing. And I'd rather not name, names. I'm morally obliged to keep my sources anonymous."

"A hit-man with morals!" John sniggered. "Isn't that a contradiction of terms?"

"You really are a cretin, aren't you," Tony said. Then he turned to Mary. "The point is, I can't go asking these people questions. They're not your regular thugs, they're professionals. They run a tight ship, and they don't like inconsistencies. Just like any other business, reputation is everything. They'd rather take me out, rather than risk their integrity."

John shivered. Tony made killing sound like a legitimate business.

"But isn't there anything you can do?" Mary asked.

Tony stood up and paced the floor a moment, finally stopping in front of Sylvia. "I can try. But I can't guarantee anything. I'm sure that my agent's really pissed with me right now. There may even be a hit out on me, but if you get hold of some heavy duty cash I may be able to make this go away for now. But these guys will take a lot of persuading, so that means a shitload of cash. Maybe if I tell them I'm retiring, disappearing, I can pull it off."

"No problem," Sylvia said.

"But even so. You still need to find out who's behind this, because odds are, they will try again. And I still think the answer lies with a..hole here," he said, turning to John.

"OK John, think back," Mary said. "Have there been any strange characters hanging around lately?"

"Present company excepted, no!"

"What about Sally? What does she do with herself all day?"

"I really don't know," he said. "I guess what all middle class suburban women do - shop. She's been busy with the remodel. She goes to some reading ...some writing group or something. Occasionally, she helps the local church to raise money. Help the Aged, I think, Aids. I really don't know."

"She helps with Soup Kitchens," Sylvia said.

"What about this reading group?"

"It's a neighborhood reading group, run by Helen Pearce," John said. "There's a Joan ...Joan Pringle ..."

Mary produced a notebook and pen from her purse and started writing down the names.

"There's a Marie, and a Rachael, but I don't know their last names," he added.

"Marie Thomson," Sylvia said. "No idea what Rachael's last name is."

"Do you know any of these women personally?" Mary asked.

"Why would I?" John snatched a glance at Sylvia.

Mary shot him a suspicious look. "No reason, just wanted to know if you knew any of them. Background information. That's all."

"Well in the past, Sally and I have spent the occasional evening at the Pearce's, Frank and Helen Pearce. But that's about it." He shrugged his shoulders casually. But he felt his face heat up.

"You're hiding something!" Sylvia said. They all stared at him.

"Really, I don't think it's relevant."

"Go on," Mary prompted.

"Well, Helen and I had this ...thing together."

"You had an affair with Sally's best friend?" Sylvia said incredulously.

John turned to her. "She kept pursuing me. She kept teasing me in front of Sally. You know a nudge here and a wink there, while Sally's back was turned. It got out of hand. I tried to put a stop to it. But she said she would tell Sally if I tried to break it off."

"Ugh," Sylvia turned away in disgust.

"She just threw herself at me."

"Oh, please!" Sylvia exclaimed.

"It was a long time ago. We'd just bought the house and Sally had just given up work. I got the promotion I wanted and everything was going great. Then Helen came on to me. It just kinda happened. I know it was stupid. And I really did love Sally back then."

Sylvia turned around to confront him. "So when did the affair end?" she asked, her hands on her hips.

"Well from my point of view, about two years ago, but, well, Helen took a long time to get the message. She just wouldn't let go."

"You mean you're still seeing her?" Sylvia asked.

"No, No, not exactly. Towards the end, she'd call me at work. She was just playful; liked telephone sex. Occasionally, she'd threaten to tell Sally about our affair. So I'd take her out to dinner, somewhere discreet."

"Do you think she could be our person?" Tony asked.

"No! No, she's harmless," John said "Totally delusional, but harmless."

"When was the last time you heard from her?" Mary quizzed.

"I bumped into her and Frank a couple of months ago. I was with Leslie at a restaurant downtown. They were celebrating their wedding anniversary. I told them that Leslie and I were having a business meeting, but I could tell that Helen hadn't bought it. I haven't seen or heard from her since. I just figured she'd finally got the message that we were through." John shrugged his shoulders. "End of story."

"She didn't call?" Tony asked.

"Nope. Not once."

"Huh!" Tony said, "Don't you think that's kinda odd. That someone obsessed with you for that long, just suddenly dropped you like that?"

"Frankly, I haven't given it a second thought. I'm just relieved she'd stopped harassing me." There was silence a moment. "Look guys," John continued. "I don't think she's behind this. She's probably got her claws into someone else by now. Like I said, she's harmless."

"Really!" Tony said. "And you know enough about psychopaths to give an informed opinion like that, huh?"

"Well I didn't until today," John sneered. He thought Helen was saner than all of them put together.

"I agree, it makes no sense!" Sylvia said. "Why now? Why would she attempt to kill Sally now that he's shacking up with someone else. If anyone she'd go after this Leslie. Sounds to me, like she's finally let go."

Tony turned to John. "Does that sound like Helen? Would she just let go, after seeing you with another woman?"

"From what you've said, she sounds like a very vindictive person," Mary added.

"Well, yes," John agreed.

"So why hasn't she told Sally about seeing you with another woman?" Mary asked. "Would you have expected Helen to have been so congenial?"

John thought it through. He recalled the day when he had tried to call off their affair. When he told her he didn't want to see her anymore. She'd flipped between being angry and not comprehending what he was saying, like some crazy person. So he made up an excuse, blamed it on circumstances. He told her he couldn't live the quality of life he wanted without Sally's money. Helen said she understood, that she would wait for him, as long as it was she he ultimately wanted. Before Helen had seen him with Leslie, he knew that Helen thought she was the only woman for him. So why hadn't she told Sally about his affair with Leslie?

"Think about it. If I were her," Mary said. "I mean, if I were trying to have Sally murdered, I wouldn't want to tell Sally about John's affair with Leslie. That would risk Sally telling someone, and involve myself as well. The last thing a perpetrator wants is attention."

Good point thought John. Everyone turned to look at him.

"I think we should have a talk to this Helen," Tony said.

"But where would she get that kind of money?" Sylvia asked.

"Look, I'm not going to sit here speculating any longer," Tony stood up. "This Helen's a real possibility and I would really like to get on with the rest of my life!"

"But what if we're wrong?" Sylvia said, "Sally would be devastated if she thought that I had wrongly accused Helen of something like that. She thinks the world of her."

Mary went over to her. "Well even if she didn't plan to have Sally murdered. She's hardly a friend I would want to keep."

"Sylvia, I need that money, like yesterday," Tony instructed. She headed towards the door.

"I'll contact my agent in Chinatown. And Mary! I want you to look after Casanova here," he added.

"Yes, but what we need is to take Helen out of the picture altogether," Mary said. Everyone stopped in their tracks.

"You mean, kill her," Tony asked, incredulously.

"No. No, of course not." she replied. "I've got an idea. But we'll need him to co-operate," she said turning to John.

"Oh no.! No ...no! I'm not getting involved in anything," he said.

"Don't worry," Sylvia said confidently. "He'll do it."

21

She was stuck in the old oak tree in her parent's garden. Beneath her, Ellie rolled about the lawn in fits of laughter. "Go get daddy," Sally said, laughing.

This isn't real. This is a dream.

The branch cracked. *I'm going to fall.* "Ellie go, get dad!" she screamed. Ellie scrambled to her feet and ran into the house. Sally crawled along the branch as fast as she could. The branch snapped. She screamed, and fell through the air.

Her eyes sprang open. She heard giggling from outside. *Kids.* Disoriented, she pushed herself upright, peeling her warm body from the leather couch. *Ouch!* She massaged the knotted muscles at the base of her head. *I must've fallen asleep while waiting for Mom to come home last night.* The clock above the mantelpiece read 7:56 am. *Where on earth is she?*

Sally shot up from the couch. Her head spun, her vision ebbing and flowing. Dizzy, she lost her balance and fell back down onto the couch. Loud, heart-pumping hammerings pummeled the inside of her head. She cowered, holding her head in her hands; the alcohol from the day before reaping its revenge.

Much slower this time, Sally got to her feet and glided to the kitchen, keeping her head as steady as possible. Squatting in front of the four drawer cabinet she pulled out the bottom one containing medication. Looking straight ahead, she rummaged through it, feeling for the bottle of aspirin. She brought a couple of bottles up to her face, before locating the right one, then slowly stood up.

After fighting the childproof top, she popped a couple of the tablets into her mouth, throwing her head back as she swallowed. The sudden movement made her vision flicker, like a movie stuck between two frames. She clung to the counter, trying to focus on the telephone, waiting for her brain to re-anchor and her stomach to settle. *John, the swine, he hadn't come home again last night either.* She picked up the telephone and speed dialed their apartment. It rang five times then the answer machine cut in. *Oh, to hell with him.* She slammed down the phone, flinching from the sound.

Again, she thought about her mother. *Why hadn't she called? What if she's had an accident?* Convinced that her mother was lying somewhere injured, she picked up the telephone again, this time to call the police. *But what shall I say? That my sixty-year-old mother had stayed out all night? I'd sound ridiculous. Besides, they'd want to know where she'd gone. And I don't have a clue. Or do I?*

After replacing the handset a second time, she carefully made her way to her mother's room. Inside, she spotted a

221

black leather book lying on the bedside table. As hoped, it was her mother's old address and telephone book. Feeling intrusive, yet at the same time feeling perfectly justified, she paged through it, searching for her mother's friend's telephone number. She found no listing for Grace under her maiden name, so continued leafing through the rest of the book. Sally didn't recognize any of the names; she realized that her mother's life was a complete mystery.

A few possible listings for Grace were G. Pilkington, a G. Mason and a G. S. Stanton, but none had a Bay Area dialing number. *This is probably out of date anyway, she's probably got the number on her cell phone. Maybe I'm overreacting. Perhaps Grace's daughter hadn't made it down from Seattle yet and mom felt obligated to stay the night.* Her mother was so independent Sally supposed it wouldn't occur to her to let her know she was staying out.

Deciding she had little choice but to wait until she heard from her mother, Sally replaced the address book on the bedside table. Turning to leave, her toe knocked against something underneath the bed. Bending over, she spotted her mother's suitcase. Her head swirled. The case, the bed, and the floor rippled towards her in waves. She stumbled backward against the wall. Worried that she might fall, she slid down it, until she was safely parked on the floor. Focusing on the suitcase, waiting for her vision to steady, she felt a strong compulsion to open it. The address book revealed just how little she knew of her mother, maybe she could learn more from the contents of her suitcase. Without further reflection, Sally pulled the suitcase towards her, flicked open the latches, and pushed back the lid.

As expected, it was packed with neatly folded clothes. Sally stacked them beside the case on the carpet. There was nothing of interest; T-shirts, pants, a sweater, underwear, a dress, a couple of pairs of shoes, and a blue sweatshirt, all the makings of a week's vacation. Feeling foolish, she began to repack the case. But when she picked up the sweater, a faux leopard-skin wallet dropped from it. She turned it over in her hand, surprised that her mother would own something so cheap and tasteless. *Why didn't she have it with her?*

She opened it up and immediately a folded piece of yellow paper dropped into her lap. Inside the wallet, there was a clear plastic compartment holding a driving license. Although she was looking at it upside down it was obvious that it wasn't her mother's photograph. She turned it around and saw the image of a young, dark-haired woman called Leslie Meadows. *What's mom doing with someone else's wallet?* Perhaps, she thought, her mother had found it and hadn't had time to return it. *But then, why was it wrapped in a sweatshirt and buried at the bottom of her suitcase?*

Sally placed the wallet on top of the sweater, picked up the piece of paper in her lap, and unfolded it. Written in black ink, she read John and Leslie's Bank of America No: 6784 595734 4984. Suddenly feeling intrusive, she refolded the note and slipped it back inside the wallet. She wrapped the sweater around it and carefully repacked the case. She closed the suitcase and slid it back underneath the bed, mindful that her meddling had created more questions than answers.

Sally sat back against the wall. A tornado of thoughts whipped through her mind. Surely there was a simple explanation. Of course, her mother wouldn't have stolen it. She was rolling in money. *But then why did she have it?* It seemed the more information she gleaned about her mother the less she comprehended. But then after Joan and Marie's revelations this week, she no longer had confidence in her ability to understand anything, anymore.

Feeling she'd already opened Pandora's box, Sally dragged the case out a second time. Finding the wallet, she pulled out its contents from behind the woman's driving license. Amongst a mountain of sales receipts, she found credit cards, business cards, a couple of grocery lists, and about $65 in cash. Finding them of no interest, she shoved them all back. On the other side, she found the folded piece of paper, a tiny calculator, and a photograph. "John!" she gasped. It was her John. She re-read the details on the yellow piece of paper. John and Leslie's bank account number. "No, no, no John," she moaned. Although it had crossed her mind that he might be having an affair, she was devastated by the reality.

Someone was knocking on her front door. Filled with adrenalin, Sally jumped to her feet. *Mom!* She went to answer the door clutching the wallet.

"John having an affair? Where did you get that idea?" she imagined her mother saying. Her mother would explain everything and scold her for rummaging through her belongings. Sally yanked open the door.

Andy!

His broad smile quickly faded, as his face met hers.

"Are you OK?" he asked.

"Yes, yes I'm fine. I've… I've, got the most dreadful headache."

"I've come," he said, shifting awkwardly from one foot to the other. "Well, I've come to pick up the rest of my tools. They're in the backyard," he added cautiously.

She held the door wider, inviting him inside. He stepped gingerly into the hallway and she closed the door after him. She strutted to the kitchen, dropped the wallet on the counter, then slid open the patio door. Andy was riveted to the spot in the hallway.

"Your tools?" she prompted.

"Oh yes…"

She smelled his distinctive woody scent, as he brushed past her and stepped into the backyard. He squatted and quickly threw his tools into his bag, while Sally briskly wiped away the film of tears blurring her vision.

Andy stepped inside. "I'll get going then."

She nodded yes.

"Well, goodbye," he said.

She only managed to mouth goodbye, since her throat refused to give life to words. Her eyes filled again. All she could see were patches of him, his blue jeans and dark brown T-shirt, increasing in size. She looked away, embarrassed that he'd come closer.

"What's happened?" he asked.

She tried to blink away her tears, but instead they tumbled down her cheeks. "I've just found out that John's having an affair."

"What? Are you sure?"

She nodded yes and cried openly. He dropped his tool bag and placed an arm around her. Impulsively, she fell onto his chest.

"I'm so sorry, Sally," He felt so comforting. He tried to pull away, but she gripped him firmer, locking her arms behind his back.

Feeling his body tense, she let him go and went to the box of tissues on the kitchen counter. "I'm sorry," she said. "You must think I'm such an idiot." She blew her nose and dabbed her eyes dry.

"No, no I don't. I just can't believe he could be such a prick!"

She smiled weakly at him. "I feel such a fool. I can't really blame him. He didn't want to move here in the first place. He hates Fenton. I pushed him. We should've stayed in the city."

"But that doesn't give him an excuse to have an affair." Andy, moved closer. "Sally, it's not your fault!"

She remembered how perceptive he had been about her family. He had sensed some anomaly between herself and her mother, and again, he was embarrassingly right. Suddenly, she felt silly trying to rationalize John's behavior. Of course, it was inexcusable. "You're right. This is not my fault." She blotted her eyes. "So did you get us right?"

Andy frowned, looking puzzled.

"Your personality profile on us. You've finished the job, moving on. So what do you make of us?" He reddened and turned away. She realized that she'd embarrassed him. "I'm sorry. You don't need this." A rogue tear fell down her cheek.

226

He plucked a tissue from the box and handed it to her. "I know one thing. I know that you are a nice person, who deserves to be treated better than this."

"I am, I do?" she said, dabbing her face.

"Yes, of course you do. Everyone deserves to be happy."

He's right I do. I didn't ask for much. I only wanted what was best for us. I've put my heart and soul into this marriage. I never even considered whether I was happy, as long as he was. Mom's right, I've been trying too hard. I should be happy now. Not when the remodel is done. Not when John had come around to living in Fenton. Not sometime in the future, but right now! She glanced at the wallet and realized that his affair shouldn't have been such a surprise. She went over all the strange conversations they'd had in the past; credit card items, his overtiredness and irritability, his general behavior, which with hindsight made perfect sense. *He must have resented every moment he'd spent with me.*

A stream of contrasting emotions ran through her mind. Hurt, betrayal, anger, bereavement followed closely by a renewal, a beginning, and new possibilities. Why so quickly? Deep down she had known for some time that John had left her, maybe not physically but emotionally. She'd already experienced the negative emotions that went along with it without really being cognizant of it. Now that denial was no longer an option she was more than ready to pick up the pieces.

"I know it's hard to believe right now," Andy said "But you'll get through it. You need to get out more. Have some fun."

She stared into his piercing blue eyes and remembered how he made her feel in the garden the day before.

"You think so," she said, moving closer. "What do you suggest," she challenged.

He reddened.

She put her arms around his neck and placed her head on his chest. She inhaled his musky, woody smell, and listened to the rapid beat of his heart.

She felt his hands gently touch hers, unlinking them from his neck. "You look tired," he said. He seemed to be struggling to find the right words. "You should get some rest." He placed a hand in the small of her back and guided her to the couch. She lay down. He placed a pillow beneath her head, and grabbed the throw from the back of the couch, gently tucking it around her.

"Do you know you have the most startling blue eyes?" Although it didn't seem possible, he reddened even more. She stroked the side of his face, it felt soft and rough at the same time, his soft expression neutralizing the stubble on his chin.

He pulled her hand away from his face. "This isn't a good idea. You're upset. And I should go."

"Of course you should, but I don't want you to. Do you want to go?"

Andy didn't answer. Feeling foolish, she turned away, trying to think of a face-saving way out. Then he kissed her cheek. She turned to face him, his warm breath lightly floated across her face and then his lips touch hers. His kisses were light and experimental, testing her response. She returned his kisses firmly, reassuringly. Her body rose with excitement, a warm glow swept through her.

He pulled away the cover and moved on top of her. Frantically, she moved her hands up and down his back, his neck, his head and his buttocks.

"This is insane," he said, panting, kissing her face, her eyelids, her neck.

"I know," she whispered. "But don't stop."

The telephone rang. She heard her mother's voice. Amid the whirlwind of emotions Sally didn't hear her message but felt relieved she was alright.

22

It was 10:00 am when John finally pulled onto Helen's driveway. He'd spent the night in a small seedy motel room in Ashwood with Sylvia and her co-conspirators while they planned their next move – or more precisely, planned his next move.

After calling Helen, he'd topped up his car with gas, ate a Happy Meal, and even though he hadn't smoked for 15 years, bought a pack of cigarettes, all to delay the inevitable. He shifted his car into park and slumped over the steering wheel, mulling over the events that had led up to this moment. *Why hadn't I seen this coming? Risk analysis is my job, for Christ's sake! Sally finding out about my indiscretions – covered. My company firing me – covered. Leslie running out of patience – covered. But shootings! Hit men! Abduction! This is fucking insane.* For the first time in his life he felt powerless, as though some higher force was pulling the strings and he could do nothing about it.

Lifting his head from the steering wheel, he spotted Helen by her window. She smiled and waved enthusiastically at

230

him. He snatched the key from the ignition and was about to jump out of the car when he caught a glimpse of himself in the rearview mirror. He tilted it toward him. His red, sore eyes looked lost in the puffy skin surrounding them and the bruising to the left side of his nose, compliments of Sylvia, had turned an interesting shade of blue-green. Angling his face upward, he could see that his facial muscles had sagged, leaving deep vertical lines down his cheeks. He looked 20 years older than he did the same time yesterday. But then who wouldn't, he reasoned, considering what he'd been through during the past 48 hours. Rampant sex that a 20 year old would have been proud of, followed by several hours of interrogation by an unbalanced contract killer. *Jesus!*

John clambered from his car, slammed the door shut and approached the house with as much enthusiasm as a condemned man walking to his execution.

How did that cow of a mother-in-law talk me into this? If she didn't tell Sally about my philandering, she wasn't completely stupid, she'd have found out sooner or later! I should've told Sylvia to go to hell.

"Half a million John, how does that sound?" Sylvia had taunted. She had him over a barrel. She knew his career was over at Smithfield Price and he was desperate for money. Furthermore, he knew that Mary was right about him being the prime suspect in the shooting. And once the papers started making innuendos, Harrison would fire him on the spot and his reputation would be beyond repair. Yes now, more than ever, he needed money.

The door opened and Helen rushed at him. "Oh John. I've missed you so much!" She threw herself at him with so much fervor that he almost toppled over. She clung to him

231

like a leech, depleting him of the small amount of energy he'd managed to muster on the way over.

"Hey, hold on," he said, peering furtively over his shoulder. "Someone might see us!" He maneuvered them both inside, and kicked the door shut behind him. He unlinked her arms from around his neck and smiled weakly at her, limited by his withered facial muscles and the overwhelming anxiety of the task before him.

Helen's hair was loosely tied on top of her head, a few seductive strands dangled around her neck. She wore a short, black, tight-fitting dress and black high heels – very '80s. John became acutely aware of the disparity between their ages. *How can she think I'd still be interested in her?*

"I knew you'd come back to me. I knew you'd eventually tire of that silly bitch." She kissed him long and hard. He pushed her away, annoyed by her offensive reference to Leslie. "And frankly, you couldn't have timed it better."

He was surprised that she hadn't noticed his displeasure, but then again, she seemed so excited she probably wouldn't have registered a major earthquake. Nevertheless, he had to contain his emotions, play along, until he got what he had come for.

"What's happened to your nose?" she asked.

"Oh," he said, touching it. "A door swung back into me. It's fine."

"Let me see. I'll go and get something for it."

"No Helen, it's fine. Please don't fuss!"

"Oh, OK grumpy." She turned on her heels and briskly headed for the kitchen. "We have to celebrate!" Helen shouted over her shoulder. He wiped the wet kiss away from

232

his mouth, admiring the back of her legs. She still had the best legs he'd ever seen.

"Celebrate? Celebrate what?"

"You just make yourself comfortable!" She shouted from the kitchen. John frantically scanned the room looking for the telephone. "I hope you still like Veuve Clicquot?" she added.

"Yes! Yes, I do!" He spotted the phone on a small table at the far end of the couch. He picked up the receiver and quickly dialed the number, all the time listening to the sounds coming from the kitchen. The line seemed to take forever to connect. He heard Helen pop the cork off the champagne. *Come on, come on.* Perspiration seeped through his brow. At last the line rang. It answered immediately.

"Hello?" Mary said.

"I'm here," he whispered. He placed the receiver down carefully, slightly off the hook so that the line was still connected.

"Where's that damned knife?" He heard Helen opening and slamming drawers. "Oh, this will have to do."

John jumped onto the couch, laid his arm across the back of it, and set his feet on the coffee table, trying to appear relaxed.

Helen returned with a tray holding two flute glasses, a bottle of champagne, a cake, plates, and a sharp knife.

What is all this?

Helen placed the tray on the coffee table in front of them. She was glowing, obviously over the moon about something. She kicked off her shoes and knelt next to him on the couch, then undid his tie, murmuring an inane tune and

233

smiling like a Cheshire cat. He stared at her mouth, her self-assuredness reminded him of Sylvia's smug grin. He was tempted to leave. Just walk out and be done with it. *But the money?* Would Leslie support him while he got back on his feet? This was something he hadn't had time to consider.

Feeling uncomfortable, he adjusted his seating, leaving him inadvertently staring down Helen's cleavage. Her breasts rose and fell with excitement and vitality.

"So what's this all about?" he asked.

"Relax John, all in good time. Let's just celebrate our reunion." She poured the champagne, picked up both glasses and handed one to him.

"To us!" she said.

"To, to us," he replied. They clinked glasses and John threw the champagne down his throat.

Helen took his glass from him and along with hers, placed them on the table. She planted short, tender kisses on his face. "John, our troubles are over."

"They are?" Her brown eyes were darker and larger than he remembered. He felt entranced.

"Yes they are." She caressed the side of his face and whispered into his ear. "We're free at last to start our lives together."

He wondered how she could've come to such a conclusion. He noticed her strange, self-satisfied expression as she started unbuttoning his shirt. He was so tired that he felt detached, that his body was there but it took too much energy for his mind to be present. Her silky cool fingers slithered across his bare chest.

"How, how do you figure that?" he gasped, suddenly springing back to the moment.

She didn't answer. Her head traveled slowly down his body stopping at the top of his trousers. His temperature zoomed to boiling point, as the friction between his senses rubbed against each other like sandpaper. His head fell back against the couch. *Oh, God, no!*

"Whoa, what do you mean Helen?" he croaked.

Still Helen didn't answer. She popped the button on his trousers and unzipped his fly before he could stop her. Automatically, his buttocks tightened. *Oh God!* His breathing became short and shallow, not from excitement but from confusion. So devoid of energy that her assault on him made his nerve endings jolt. He grabbed hold of her hand, but she held on tight.

"What do you mean, Helen?" he asked again, breathlessly.

"All in good time," she said.

He felt clammy, conscious that everything was being heard over the telephone. In a desperate attempt to take control, he bravely let go of her hand and pulled her face up to his. He kissed her. Mercifully, she relaxed her grip.

"What do you mean we're free?"

"Sally won't be bothering anyone, anymore," she said. Her eyes were closed.

John froze. *What? Had she taken the bait?* Earlier, from their motel bedroom, Tony had left a cryptic message on Helen's answer machine, implying that Sally was dead. Contrary to his accomplices' theory, John didn't believe that Helen was behind the hit and told them they were being absurd. "Well, we'll soon find out," Tony explained, as he was taking the

235

phone's handset apart. "If she didn't arrange the hit, she'll disregard the message, thinking some nutter's left it, but if she did, she'll show her hand. Tony placed an amplified auditory device in the earpiece of the phone's handset, reassembled it and placed it back on its cradle. "Hey, don't worry 'Cotton Socks'," Tony said, playfully punching his arm. "You just do your part and make sure she stays near her phone."

John kissed Helen's neck, so she couldn't see the distress he was now feeling. He realized that the only way he could get more information from her, was to maintain the charade of lovemaking. He continued kissing her and unzipped her dress. She giggled as he pulled her dress down to her waist. She unfastened her bra, and he playfully yanked it from her. She maneuvered herself down on the couch, grabbing the back of his neck, pulling him on top of her.

"Why won't she be bothering us anymore?" He felt her shudder with excitement. "What've you been up to?"

"Later," She grabbed his hand and pushed it between her thighs. "It's been a long time John."

He caressed the edge of her panties. She held onto his head and kissed him hard. He was losing ground. Furthermore, he was blatantly aware that everything could be heard over the telephone and it wouldn't take a rocket scientist to work out what they were doing.

"But what did you mean about Sally?"

"For Christ's sake, John!" Helen suddenly yelled. "What's the matter with you?" She studied his face a moment and then pushed him away. He sat up and ran his hand through his hair, realizing he'd blown it. She scampered backward to the far end of the couch. She sat up and held her dress over her front. "Don't tell me you're having second thoughts about Sally?" She eyed him suspiciously. "Not after all this time? Or is it, you'd rather be with that silly bitch at work! Is that it?"

John perspired profusely. He chastised himself for pushing the issue too soon. He should have taken it slower even if it meant having sex with her. *No, damn it. I shouldn't be here in the first fucking place!*

"So which is it?" she barked.

He glanced at her, considering his options. He could leave. *But the money? What about the money?* Could he and Leslie weather his financial situation without Sylvia's bribe, until he found another job? No, he decided. He couldn't take the risk. He'd have to see this through. "Neither," he finally said. "You've always been the best." He moved towards her. "It just took me a while to realize it." He stroked the side of her face. "It's just been a hell of a week."

Helen's expression softened. "It's OK. I understand. I'm a little stressed out myself."

He kissed her palm.

"What you need is a good screw," she said. His eyes closed involuntary. His heart palpitated. Nothing could be further from the truth, he thought.

John, however, obliged by pulling her down on the couch, pushing her comment aside and his hand between her legs, realizing that he had no alternative but to screw her into confession. He had an epiphany. It occurred to him that he was, in essence, doing this for Sally. Having sex with her best friend was going to save Sally. Life, he thought, was extremely ironic.

John pulled off her panties and threw them over his shoulder. He pulled down her dress. She raised her arms over her head, in submission. He shut his eyes and tried to evoke Leslie's image, hoping to pull off a decent screw and trying to block out the fact that his co-conspirators were probably having a good laugh on the other end of the telephone.

Helen moaned with delight and tweaked his nipple, but it was Leslie who pulled at it with her teeth. Helen took hold of his buttocks, Leslie clawed at them with her nails. Leslie bit into his neck. Leslie stuck her tongue down his ear. Leslie was with him all the time, holding onto him, pulling at his hair, scratching his back. After a couple of minutes he heard a fulfilled climatic wail. It was Helen's voice. Instinctively, John opened his eyes and pulled away from her. He lay on his back panting, reflecting on the power that Leslie's image had over him, reaffirming that she was the only woman for him.

Helen propped herself up on her elbow. "I needed that," she said panting.

He stood up and shuffled his pants back into place. He fastened his trousers and sat down next to her.

She reached over to the table and picked up her half empty glass of champagne.

"So," he said, refilling his glass. "What's my favorite girl been up to?" He felt nervous and hoped he'd picked the right moment to probe. The top half of her body was still naked. In order to keep her happy, he dipped his finger into the champagne and ran it down the middle of her chest. He felt her body rise. Her head fell back, soaking it all up.

"Sally and Frank are gone," she said.

John stopped his finger. *Frank's dead?* Helen lifted her head a little, so he continued his playfulness.

"What do you mean?" he asked with more concern than he would have liked.

Helen faced him. Her hair was disheveled, adding malice to her sharp, cold expression. The message was loud and clear; playtime's over. She shot up from the couch and placed her glass on the table. "I'll just be a minute," she said, disappearing down the hallway to the bathroom while slipping her arms into her dress. He buttoned his shirt and tucked the tail ends into his trousers.

Moments later, Helen returned from the bathroom. She pulled a cigarette from a packet on the fireplace and struck a match. After lighting and sucking hard on the cigarette, she blew a fierce shaft of blue smoke into the air. "Remember the old days, the plans we made, the holidays, and the adventures we talked about? And remember how you said that money was wasted on Sally, that she and you never did anything fun with it? That money was invented for the likes of us?"

Yes, he nodded. After sex, they'd often fantasized about buying a house in the Caribbean, or buying a yacht and sailing the world. But the thought of him spending the rest of his life with her, sent a cold chill down his spine. He would drown in her pandering and possessiveness. Besides she was almost 10 years older and already starting to look a bit ropey. He hadn't thought she'd taken him that seriously.

She took another drag of her cigarette and blew it sharply towards the ceiling. "And do you recall me saying that money was nothing to me, that I would live with you regardless. But you can't live without money, can you? And I knew you'd never do anything about it." She turned to the fireplace and stubbed her cigarette out on the stone mantelpiece. "So I did it for you. And I took care of Frank as well."

"You did what!" he said. John couldn't believe his ears.

"Think about it," she said, turning to face him again. "It's the perfect crime. No one knows about us. The police can't possibly link us, because we genuinely haven't been seeing each other."

She's crazy! He was pretty certain that Sally was ok, unless of course, she'd killed Sally herself that morning. *But Frank? Poor guy!* John hadn't liked the guy, but he didn't deserve to die. *Had she paid another hitman to get rid of him as well, or had she killed him herself. Why hadn't she just divorced him?*

It suddenly dawned on him that he was in the presence of a conniving madwoman and maybe even a murderer. If she had gone this far, who knew what she was capable of. And with what had been taped so far, he could also be accused of being an accessory to murder. He certainly wouldn't put it past Sylvia to use the tape against him. He felt scared but he had to keep it together.

"Are you OK? You look a little pale." He edged away from her as she sat beside him.

"Oh, it's nothing." He combed his fingers through his hair. "I'm just trying to get my head around this."

"You know me, John. I'm full of surprises." She placed a comforting arm around his shoulder. "I know it's sort of sudden, but think about it, we can be together now. We can take all those trips we talked about."

He glanced at her and smiled weakly. "Yes, I see that. But why now?"

Helen's arm fell away. She picked up her glass and paced the floor in front of him. She'd obviously expected a better reaction from him.

"Why not now? Just how long did you expect me to wait? You were never going to leave Sally, and I'd lost patience." She stopped in front of him waiting for his response. When he failed to say anything she yelled. "Did you really think I was satisfied with telephone sex? All you gave me were promises," she ranted and continued pacing the floor. "Next year, Helen, you'd say. When I've made a little more money. And then I saw you with that piece of trash at the restaurant on my wedding anniversary. Of course, I knew it wasn't a business meeting. I could tell by the way you looked at her. The way you used to look at me. I knew I could get you back, that you'd tire of that bitch. But this time, I wanted to make it permanent, no ties, no more excuses."

He wondered if they occupied the same planet. Apart from the telephone call this morning, he'd given her no reason to believe that they would be rekindling their relationship.

"But couldn't you just have divorced Frank?"

Helen stopped pacing the floor. "What! But that's what I did. What do you think I've been talking about? Oh, no, no, Frank's not dead! He's just gone."

241

Oh, thank God. John breathed a sigh of relief. "Where's he gone?"

"Oh, I don't know," she sniggered. "He's probably gone fishing somewhere. I think he'd rather fuck a fish than me."

At that moment, John could totally empathize with him.

"We'd been talking about splitting up for some time. It was all so fucking amicable. Frank is so emotionally challenged, a nuclear bomb wouldn't move him. We decided to split up last weekend. He simply loaded his things into his truck and left yesterday afternoon."

John tried to get a grip on the situation. Frank was gone, but not dead. Sally was alive, but as far as Helen knew, was dead. It was like something out of a cheesy movie. He shook his head.

"I just can't believe you did this!" he said, attempting to make it clear over the telephone line that he had no idea what she had planned.

"Oh, come on John. It's what we both wanted."

He shifted his seating, mindful of how all this sounded. It seemed the more he tried to get her to confess, the deeper she seemed to implicate him.

She sat down beside him and rubbed his knee, trying to console him. "Don't worry John, It's going to be fine! This way, you get the best of both worlds - me and the money. Think about it. Sally's money alone would set us up for life, never mind any insurance you have on her. I'm just as wound up as you are, but the most important thing now is to keep our heads. It'll be worth it in the end. You'll see."

She poured more champagne into their glasses. "Here," she said, handing him his glass.

John pensively sipped the champagne. The bubbles expanded and ran up the back of his nose, making his eyes smart. Realizing that Helen's back now faced the telephone and concerned that she might not be clearly heard, John, glass in hand, left the couch. He sipped his champagne and propped himself up against the fireplace. As hoped, she turned to face him, placing her in a better position to be heard over the telephone.

He placed his glass on mantelpiece. "So, the shooting. That was real?"

"Well, you didn't really believe that the shootings were high school kids, did you?" she said. "Although, it wasn't a bad cover. I was really surprised and disappointed when Sally turned up that night, I can tell you. But this morning I found a message on my answering machine, making it perfectly clear to me, that she's dead." She sipped her drink and swung her legs onto the couch. "Anyway, that part is taken care of. The only thing we need to be concerned with is the money. We need to come up with half a mil, and quickly. Now, I've already paid $100,000, but you'll have to come up with the rest."

As far as John was concerned, acknowledging Tony's message was a clear admission of guilt, but Helen still hadn't said outright that she had planned the murder. To seal the deal, and to get himself off the hook, he needed her to plainly say that she had hired the hit.

Although he risked her completely losing it, John decided to play tough. He needed her to talk more about the setup. "But I can't come up with that sort of money! You know what kind of financial situation I'm in."

"But you have to! This wasn't just some local thug. This was a professional, the kind who collects no matter what it takes." Helen's face reddened. "John, you do understand?"

She straightened, suddenly looking anxious. He knew that he'd stumbled upon the one thing she wasn't sure about. Would he come up with his share of the money?

"We have to pay. You do get it!" she added.

Spotting his opportunity, he challenged her further. "Four hundred thousand dollars," he said, shifting his weight. One hand gripped his hip and the other rubbed his chin, as if deliberating whether he should pay or not. "Why? Why didn't you tell me what you planned to do?"

Helen shook her head as if in disbelief. "You have to speculate to accumulate. Remember that, John. I've heard you say that hundreds of times!"

"Are you out of your mind! We're not talking about some gamble on the stock market or, or some fun at a casino - Jesus!"

"Don't yell at me! It's only a few hundred thousand! Think about the payoff. Think how rich we'll be when it all blows over!"

"Oh, and when do you suppose that will be?" he said, pacing the floor. "Did you ever consider the position you've put me in? The police will suspect me, Helen! I'm the one who's going to have to take the heat. Have you any idea what I'm going to have to go through? Oh, God! How am I going to get through this?" He pinched the top of his nose, peering at her through his fingers. She looked shell-shocked.

"God, you're such a wimp!" she yelled, shooting out of her seat. "I…I…I, Where did we…. go to?" she continued, pacing the room.

"What?"

"We're in this together, right?" she said.

"Now, hold on."

"The position I've put you in. How am I going to get through this?" She mocked.

"Helen, I'm going to be the prime suspect in the murder of my wife!" John said.

"Well, I've done all the hard work!"

"Oh, and how do you figure that?" he asked.

"Well, I arranged Sally's hit!"

Bingo!

"And it wasn't exactly a walk in the park," she continued ranting. "It was dammed right dangerous. I had to walk the streets of Chinatown asking guarded questions, worrying that someone might tip off the police or I might be attacked. It would have been easier to kill Sally myself. Anyway, after that first disastrous attempt, I've been assured that she was killed last night. So you just have to come up with the money!"

John glanced at the phone. They would have all they wanted by now. Helen turned around to see what he was looking at. He tensed. She went over to the phone and picked up the receiver.

"What's this?" She listened a moment. "Who's on the other end?"

"What?" John said, as indifferently as he could.

"What have you done? You've set me up, haven't you?" She ripped the phone from the wall and turned on him like some wild animal. Her eyes bulged, she looked crazed. "How could you? You stupid fucking jerk!"

Having accomplished what he'd been paid to do, John headed for the door.

"Oh no, you don't!" Helen picked up the butcher's knife from the table and ran in front of him, blocking his path, pointing the knife at his chest.

He held up his hands in defense. "Helen, put that down."

"You think you're so smart! You think you can just toss me aside like all the others, don't you!" She said, waving the knife to and fro.

"Helen put..the..knife down, before things get worse."

"Worse? How can things possibly get worse? I had Sally murdered! And you, you bastard. You set me up!" She pushed the knife towards his face.

He stared at the tip of the knife. *She's lost it.*

"No Helen, you're wrong," he explained as calmly as he could. "Sally's alive. The hit didn't happen. Her mother turned up and somehow contacted the hitman, and persuaded him not to go through with it. They were both on the other end of the phone. So nobody's hurt."

"Sally's still alive?" she asked incredulously, momentarily easing the knife away from his face. "But the message on the machine?"

"It was them, Sylvia and the hitman. I swear. They left that message to draw you out. So nobody's been harmed."

"Why can't she just die?" Helen said, her eyes full of rage. "She can't even do that properly."

246

She's nuts!

"And you." She pressed the tip of the knife into his cheek. "You're in on it, too, aren't you?"

"I had no choice," he pleaded, staring down at the blade. "They tried to pin it on me."

She went quiet for a moment. Then withdrew the knife from his cheek but still pointed it at him. She stared into space as though thinking it all through.

"Give me the knife, Helen." He moved his hand closer to the handle. "It's over."

"But I thought you loved me?" Tears suddenly spilled from her eyes, her body crumpled.

He glanced at the knife, then at Helen. He was so close, close enough to take it away, but also close enough to be hurt.

"Of course, I do. Give me the knife. Then we can sit down and work this out together." He went for the knife.

"No!" she shrieked. She slashed the knife across his wrist. A sharp stinging pain sliced through it. He stepped back, clutching his bleeding wrist.

"You've cut me. You've actually cut me!"

"Oh, I get it," she spat. "I go to jail, and you just walk away, right? Is that how it goes? They didn't have anything on me, did they?"

He glanced between his bloody wrist and Helen's contorted face. She didn't seem to notice what she'd done.

"You stupid bastard. We could've both gotten away with it," she yelled.

"We still can. Just listen to me. Put the knife down."

The doorbell rang.

247

She lunged forward, thrusting the knife into him. John felt the tip of the knife pierce his stomach. He looked at it protruding from his middle.

"Oh, my God. Helen!"

Pain surged through his body, as his brain registered that he'd been stabbed.

The doorbell rang again.

"Help!" he yelled. Helen pushed him backward. He lost his footing, bashed his head against the stone hearth, before falling to the ground. He heard the noise of it but didn't feel the impact; his whole consciousness was with his stomach. He felt nothing below or above it, only the pain right there, but even that was starting to numb. He couldn't feel or hear his heartbeat. He felt cold and clammy. Then, suddenly there was darkness. *Oh, God. I'm dying.*

23

Devastated by the discovery of John's affair and at the same time racked with guilt over her own infidelity, a confused and distraught Sally drove over to Helen's in search of absolution and counsel.

She turned into Helen's street and saw John's car in her driveway. *What the hell! What's he doing here?* She parked on the street. *Had he seen me with Andy through the window?* She stepped out of her car, threw her keys into her purse and walked pensively towards the house, passing John's car in a state of incredulity. *No, of course he hadn't! Besides, Helen would be the last person he'd go to if he had.* She rang the doorbell and waited. Again, she glanced at his car. *But what's he doing here? He's not home for two nights and now he's at Helens!* Annoyed, she pressed the doorbell again, this time for much longer. Above the sound of the bell, she heard a cry for help. It sounded like John.

"John! Helen! Open the door!" She pounded the door with one hand and firmly pressed the bell with her other.

Finally, the door opened, revealing a vertical strip of Helen's face.

"Thank God!" Sally said. "I thought I heard John shouting for help. Is everything alright?"

Helen didn't reply. Sally couldn't make anything out from her face because she could see so little of it.

"Helen?" she tried again. "I heard John shout for help. What's going on?" Still she didn't reply. Sally became anxious. "Helen! Answer me!" She stood on her tiptoes and into the gap above Helen's head shouted "John!"

Sally pushed the door toward her unresponsive friend. Helen backed into the hallway as she stepped inside. Helen's hair was disheveled. She seemed catatonic, staring into space like a zombie. Sally noted her black dress, then bloodstains on her legs. "You're bleeding!" She dropped her purse and scanned her friend's body. "Where are you hurt?" She clasped Helen's shoulders. "Listen to me? Where are you hurt!" She followed Helen's vacant stare into the middle of the living room. She spotted John lying on the floor by the fire with a knife protruding from his stomach and a pool of blood by his side.

"John!" Sally flew over and knelt beside him. "John! John!" she yelled, and then to Helen "Have you called an ambulance!" Sally bent over his face. His pallor was deathly white, as though all the blood had drained from him. She couldn't feel his breath on her face. She located his jugular vein and pressed firmly. Overwhelmed by her own heartbeat, she wasn't sure whether she could detect a pulse. She held her breath and tried again. This time she felt a slight pulse. But she knew he was in bad shape.

"Have you called 911!" Sally yelled again. Helen was now sitting on the couch. "For God's sake Helen, answer me! John's dying!"

"Help's on the way," she replied calmly.

Sally held John's cold, bloodstained hand. "John, it's Sally," she said, hoping he could hear. "The ambulance is on its way. Oh God, John, please don't die." Her instinct was to relieve him of his affliction. Her hand hovered indecisively over the knife, then she realized that removing it could be fatal. She shook with frustration and powerlessness.

She heard a click and looked up to see Helen calmly lighting a cigarette. She had never seen her smoke before. Thinking she was traumatized, Sally went over and squatted in front of her. "Helen, what's happened. Have you been burgled?"

Helen blew a plume of smoke into her face. Sally coughed and recoiled. She stood up and stepped out of the smoke's path. Helen chuckled and sat back into the couch, casually crossing one leg over the other.

"You really are something else," Helen sneered. She took another drag of her cigarette. "Have you always been this naive?" she said, smoke dancing from her mouth.

She's in shock. Sally slipped off her jacket and placed it around Helen's shoulders.

"You see blood on me. John is desperately clinging to life, and you assume that someone broke into the house? It's quite remarkable how deluded you are. Were you abused as a child or something? Is that it?"

Disturbed by her hostility, Sally backed away. She glanced between John and Helen, trying to internalize everything. If

251

an intruder hadn't done this, then there could only be one other explanation. "You mean, you did this to John?" she asked startled.

"Ah, the penny drops," Helen said, smiling and nodding her head. "John and I have been having an affair on and off for years." She flicked ash onto the floor.

My God, you as well? Sally glanced at John.

"In fact, it started two weeks after you moved here," Helen continued.

"Stop it!" Sally yelled, covering her ears. *Were all these years a lie?* She couldn't comprehend that John had been unfaithful even from the beginning of their marriage and with Helen?

Helen laughed. "That's it, what you don't hear can't hurt, right?"

Sally dropped her hands and searched for the telephone, realizing that if Helen had stabbed John she probably hadn't called for help. She glanced over to where the telephone usually was. Seeing it gone, she frantically scanned the room.

"Relax. The police are on their way." Helen said.

Sally eyed her suspiciously.

"If you don't believe me, call them."

Sally quickly retrieved her purse from the hallway, dug out her cell phone and dialed 911. "Ambulance, quickly, my husband's been stabbed! No. He's breathing, but only just. 1430 Westcott Drive, High Bank. Please hurry!"

She dropped the phone and knelt beside John. *No matter what he'd done, he didn't deserve to die.* "Oh God Helen, what have you done? Why?"

252

Suddenly, Helen lunged at her, grabbing her hair and pulling her head backward. Sally screamed, her hands grabbed Helen's fist trying to pry it open. "What have I done? Bitch! You did this to him!" Helen shrieked.

She pulled Sally away from John. Sally felt her scalp lift from her head. She shrieked, the pain was excruciating. One hand went to the carpet to keep her balance as she was dragged backwards across the floor. Finally, Helen let her go by throwing her against the wall. Sally curled into a fetal position, cradling her head, which stung and pulsated with pain. She felt streams of blood run down beneath her scalp. Above the buzzing in her ears, she heard Helen's angry outburst. "He never loved you, you stupid bitch! Couldn't you see that all he wanted was your fucking money? You were just a commodity! A steppingstone until something better came along," she continued, ranting and pacing in front of her.

Petrified and weeping, Sally slowly got to her feet and inched along the wall in the direction of the front door. Helen suddenly charged at her, grabbing her neck, pinning her against the wall. Sally's hands gripped Helen's. She couldn't breathe. She was choking. Helen's face twisted into a contorted snarl. "I should've told you about us years ago. It was so hard keeping it a secret. I was dying to tell you. To see the expression on your stupid fucking face!"

Helen released her. Coughing and rasping, Sally massaged her neck, while Helen continued pacing wildly. "We were made for one another. It was all going great until the fuckup at the bank, until that bitch Leslie got her claws into him." She stuck an accusing finger in Sally's face. "You've done this to him! Not me!" Traumatized, Sally started shaking. Fearing for her life, she glanced at the front door. It seemed so near but Helen was too close for her to make a run for it. She had to distract her. "Helen," she said softly, tearfully. "John's dying."

"You're pathetic. You still think he loves you? Don't you?" Helen spat.

"No. No Helen, I don't," she said, shaking her head.

"You want to know why you never got pregnant?"

What? What could she know about that?

Helen came within a couple of inches of her face. "You want to know why?" she said again, softly, tauntingly. She moved to Sally's ear and whispered, "because he'd had a vasectomy." Sally's heart sunk as though it had collapsed in on itself. She slid down the wall. She felt like she'd been kicked in the stomach.

Helen backed away. "I'd had my fill of kids. I didn't want anymore. And if you'd known John well enough, which obviously you didn't, he never wanted any."

Sally looked over at him. *All this time.* Rapid flashbacks appeared before her eyes. She visualized all the tests she'd had, the exercise programs, the anticipation between periods and the visits to her gynecologist. *"There's absolutely no reason why you shouldn't conceive,"* Dr. Hanson had said.

She watched Helen's mouth continue to disperse cruel insults, but she was no longer tuned in.

"So," Helen said, pulling Sally up with the front of her blouse. "What do you make of that? How are you going to turn that into something you can live with?"

Helen had struck her final blow. Nothing else could touch her. Well beyond pain, a calmness swept over her. She shook herself free from Helen's grasp. Turning her body away from Helen she clenched her fist and with all her might punched Helen across her face. She hit her with such ferocity that Helen stumbled, lost her footing and smashed her head against the glass coffee table, then fell to the floor.

Panting heavily, Sally looked down at the woman she'd previously regarded as her mentor. A pool of blood seeped from her head onto the white carpet where she had insisted that Sally sat on a towel a couple of days ago. *Oh dear,* Sally thought, *she's going to have a hard time getting that stain out.*

24

Ten days later Sally sat on Fred Patchett's memorial bench by the delta. A fresh cool breeze replaced the humidity of the past few weeks. A leaf from a walnut tree gently tapped her shoulder before falling to the ground, the wind relieving the trees of their remaining leaves of summer.

She surveyed the delta. Many people were exercising in one way or another. The memory of herself exercising there seemed alien, like she had simply stepped out of that body and it was still out there running. She no longer ran.

A cyclist rang his bell at a female jogger blocking his path. The woman graciously moved over to let him pass. Sally recognized the expensive running gear the woman wore, down to the same brand of running shoes she used to wear. She hoped the woman had a better grip on life than she had. Yes, life certainly looked different from Fred's bench.

"Hi," said a voice from behind. She closed the notebook in her lap, as Andy, parked himself beside her.

"I'm glad you phoned," he said. "I've been trying to get in touch. Every time I turn on the TV, I see the house. I've been around a few times, but nobody's been there."

It was the first time that she had seen him completely dust free. His hair seemed blonder and curlier than usual. His whole appearance sharper, more defined. Smiling at him, she slipped her arm through his and faced the bay. "I've been staying with a friend, trying to keep a low profile."

"You've cut your hair. It looks good."

"Oh, thanks," she said, touching it. "I needed a change. Thought I'd start from the outside, you know?"

"So how are you?" he asked, concerned.

"I'm fine," she said, facing him squarely. He was frowning. "Really. I'm doing OK." She squeezed his arm appreciatively.

A small yacht motored out of the harbor. Sally remembered how her father had once wanted a boat, but her mom had firmly opposed it, saying that he was far too clumsy to be anywhere near water. *Typical of mother,* she thought laughing inside. But at the time it hadn't seemed so funny. One of Sally's biggest frustrations had been her mother's dominance over her father. He always backed down if her mother disapproved of anything he wanted to do. But having got closer to her over the past couple of weeks, she realized that her mother's tight reign over him was about her own insecurity. She supposed everyone had a vulnerable side. Her father had been a dreamer, a born adventurer. She could well imagine him taking off on some adventure, never to be seen again. She sensed these conflicting traits in herself, her past craving security and her present yearning freedom from it.

"All this business seems to have put Fenton on the map," Andy said brightly. "The story's even hit the national news. And I'm a bit of a celebrity down at 'The Hole,' being acquainted with the victim and his wife. Everyone wants to know about you and John. By the way, how's he doing?"

"He's fine, as far as I know. I expect he'll be in the hospital for at least another week. Leslie, the woman he'd been seeing, is with him. I really don't think there's much point in me visiting." A gust of wind blew a lock of hair into her mouth. She shook it away. "We're getting divorced you know."

She hadn't seen John since the day he'd been rushed to hospital. Of course, she'd accompanied him in the ambulance and stayed until his condition stabilized. But he'd never regained consciousness, while she'd been there. Around 8:30 pm that evening, a nurse came to the room and told her that a young woman was anxious to see him. Sally immediately recognized Leslie from her driving license, when she stepped into the hallway to meet her. But from Leslie's calm demeanor, it was obvious that she had no idea who Sally was. Then Leslie's face turned crimson as it dawned on her who she must be.

Sally put her out of her misery. "He's all yours," she said, plucking Leslie's wallet from her purse and handing it to her. "And good luck to you!" she yelled over her shoulder as she marched down the hallway, out of the hospital, and John's life forever.

"It seems John had been having affairs throughout our entire marriage?" she continued telling Andy. "Helen, the woman who tried to kill him had been carrying on with him since we moved to Fenton, and I thought she was my best friend." Helen had been released from hospital and taken into custody the very next day.

"Somehow my mother, oh God, I feel so bad about her now." Sally regretted all the wasted years between them. She blamed herself for not confronting her mother about their relationship years ago. Now there was so little time left for them to enjoy each other. "Somehow she found out about Helen's plan," she continued. "She and some friends taped Helen's confession and handed it to Detective Darnell. I think he's having second thoughts about moving here now," she chuckled.

"What are you going to do?" Andy asked.

Sally's attention turned back to the yacht. Its sails flapped erratically as it motored through the gap in the sea wall. Then the crew winched its sails; the yacht heeled a moment then picked up speed, gliding through the water like a seagull skimming the surface. Sally would remember this moment, the day that she journeyed into unchartered waters.

Glancing at the harmless white clouds racing across the sky, then at the boat and its crew, she became aware of life's and continuous motion and how busy it was. Before the shooting, yesterday would have been the same as today and today would have been the same as tomorrow. But that was because of John. He had been the center of her world and she had been a mere extension of it. Willingly, she'd surrendered her distinctiveness preferring safety and security, putting John's needs before her own, and vacating the need to live her own life. Time seemed endless then. But now that she was alone, the world seemed much bigger and faster. She felt both excited and scared at the prospect of facing the world alone, but she knew she had to, if she was going to have any life at all. What a pity, she thought, that she was starting her journey just as her mother was ending hers.

"Sally?"

"Hmm?" she replied.

"What are you going to do?" Andy asked again.

"Well. I'm selling the house. A friend of mine's having another baby and needs the extra room." Marie had completely lost it with Kent. She'd told him that the only way she would stay with him and go through with the pregnancy was if he agreed to have a vasectomy. At first, he'd baulked at the idea and so to prove that she was serious she took off and left him with the kids for four days. Marie said he was so relieved when she returned he would have agreed to castration had she asked him.

Joan's divorce had been swift, and amazingly, she had never looked back. She'd been lucky enough to engage part-time employment with an image consultancy, capitalizing on her years at finishing school and her knowledge of high-end fashion.

Sally thought it strange how her friends' lives had been turned upside-down at the same time as her own. It was as though that bullet had ricocheted around all of them.

"Actually, Marie needs something bigger, but at least it's better than what she's got," she continued. "It never really was mine anyway. Oh, and while we're on the subject, can you give this to Mike?" she said, handing him a couple of hundred dollar bills. "Tell him I expect the plants to stay where they are!"

"But where are you going?" Andy asked, clutching the money and looking perplexed.

"Back East, to where I left off. I'm actually on my way to the airport," she said, checking her watch. "My mother wanted to come with me, but I persuaded her to go to a wedding she'd been invited to in Greece. Besides, I need to be alone for a while.

"This is all a bit sudden isn't it?" he said.

"That's not the way I see it. It's been far too long in the making. I've spent all my life avoiding being me. I don't think I've ever made any decisions, you know any important ones. And I'm so incapable of making them now, I can't even make up my mind what kind of ice cream to buy! Like you said, I need to start living, before it's too late."

"Don't take any notice of me," he said. "I'm full of it. Look, lots of marriages break up. I don't think it's necessary for you to just take off like this. Besides it wasn't your fault John played around."

"Oh, but you're wrong! I let it happen. Most people would have figured out at some point that their marriage was in trouble. But not me!" She shook her head. "No. This is as much my fault, as John's. I was only too happy to let him do this to me. I'm not going to do that again. And for my own sanity, I need to be on my own right now and probably for a long time."

Andy unlinked his arm from hers. She felt compelled to pacify him, to explain further, but then irritation suddenly percolated inside her. *Here we go again! No, damn it, this is my time! Besides, I don't owe him anything.*

His cheek muscle quivered as he stared stubbornly ahead, obviously upset. It wasn't his fault. He had, after all, played a part in this.

Sally nudged him. "Thank you,' she said.

"What for?" He asked, his piercing blue eyes betraying a glimmer of hope.

"For being there, at the right time."

"We…"

"No, Andy there's no we!"

He paused a moment, searching her eyes as though trying to find the words to persuade her. Finally, he nodded acceptance and faced the water.

"The sex was pretty good though," he said.

"Yes it was!" They both laughed.

———————————

Mary looked into Tony's eyes with apprehension. Tony looked into her eyes with total love and adoration. The Mediterranean sun looked down on them kindly, as the two exchanged their wedding vows. Mary wore a short, cream, lace dress and held a simple bouquet of pink and white roses. Tony wore a formal, dark-blue suit and tie.

They stood on a bluff overlooking Onos Beach in Skiathos, the aqua sea gently caressing the timeless sand below. Picture perfect, thought Sylvia.

"I now pronounce you husband and wife," ended the priest. Immediately cheers and applause broke the small crowds silence and pieces of confetti flew into the air, over the newlyweds. The colored pieces of paper flirted with the sunlight, drifting slowly and elegantly to the ground. Their magic only noticed by Sylvia and a couple of young children, the latter trying to catch as many pieces as they could.

Tony and Mary reveled in the congratulations bestowed on them by the villagers and by Tony's newly discovered extended family, who, when all said and done, looked a dubious lot. He would feel right at home here, thought Sylvia. *Home*, Sylvia pondered. *Another delusion.*

Sylvia felt as though she were standing outside a huge translucent glass bulb containing life, as she had always known it. At first, she wondered whether this was part of the dying process, that her mind had already become detached from the world. And still she wasn't sure.

But from her unique position, she felt that she was seeing life as it really was. No longer participating in life's dramas, she could clearly see them play out in the people around her. A common thread seemed to be an insatiable desire to become someone more than they were or become monstrously wealthy, as if their happiness depended on it. She admitted that she had been that way too. But now stripped of ego, she knew that all the dreams and dramas didn't matter. Although she still believed in taking an active role in one's own destiny, she had also come to realize that happiness was an option. That pleasure or displeasure could be controlled by one's mind and had little to do with the material world. She thought it sad and wasteful how people were so absorbed in their desires that they often missed the beauty, the moments of pure bliss that surrounded them every moment of the day.

The children get it, thought Sylvia, as she watched them jump around in their own little carefree world. The only time that she had truly been in the moment was when she had thrown caution to the wind and went on her adventure to England. She felt her cheeks lift into a familiar smile when she was reminded of it but then she thought of Sally.

Sylvia wanted to comfort her after returning home from the hospital the day John had been stabbed. But she struggled to find the right sentiment. She wanted to tell Sally that none of it really mattered, that she should get on with her life and not give the past a second thought. It was spent, over. But then, no-one in their right mind, unless they were walking in Sylvia's shoes, would accept negating the last five years of their lives with a few short sentences of wisdom. Consequently, hardly a word was exchanged between them for a couple of days. It was apparent that Sally had her own demons to contend with, just as Sylvia had. It occurred to her that one's conviction to 'reality' was measured by the amount of time one has left on the earth. It, therefore, became impossible for her to give Sally any useful advice and so instead she said nothing. Sylvia had an inkling that life's journey was about finding one's own way out of the bubble or, as in Sylvia's case, life just kicked you out.

"Turn around, guys!" Sylvia shouted. Tony and Mary faced her, with smiles of sheer happiness. She quickly raised her camera to her eye and captured the image with a flick of her finger. An old lady dressed in black came up from behind shouting loudly at her in Greek. The woman snatched the camera from Sylvia and waved her hand vigorously, indicating that she should stand with the newlyweds. Sylvia stepped between the couple, placing one arm around Tony's waist and the other around Mary's, thinking what wonderful devices cameras were for capturing a moment, a moment when everything seemed perfect.

"Chaze! Chaze!" shouted the woman.

"Chaze!" they laughed.

Click.

www.ingramcontent.com/pod-product-compliance
Lightning Source LLC
Chambersburg PA
CBHW050019180626
46810CB00002B/492